Cecil Browne was born in St Vincent and the Grenadines, SVG. He emigrated to England to join his parents in the seventies. He was Head of Maths in a Further Education College for ten years. Passionate about Caribbean music, history, cricket, literature and folklore, his cricket short story, *Coming Off the Long Run*, was published in *So Many Islands*, an anthology of stories from the Caribbean, Mediterranean, Indian and Pacific Oceans, in 2017. He is married, with two daughters.

BOOKS BY CECIL BROWNE

The Moon is Following Me
'Browne has a gift for creating memorable and appealing
characters and for placing them in unlikely situations.'
Maeve Tynan, *Wasafiri*

'Browne delights in making his characters swim against the currents
of their lives. He couples this with a deft turn of phrase and an eye
for detail that makes otherwise commonplace moments sparkle.'
Ann Morgan, *St Vincent & the Grenadines: journeys*

Feather Your Tingaling
'Browne's use of folklore as a key thematic tool laces each
story with an element of other-timeliness as well as
contemporaneous relevance.'
Natsayi Sithole, *Wasafiri*

CASSIE P
CARIBBEAN PI

Cecil Browne

Matador
9 Priory Business Park,
Wistow Road, Kibworth Beauchamp,
Leicestershire. LE8 0RX
Tel: 0116 279 2299
Email: books@troubador.co.uk
Web: www.troubador.co.uk/matador
Twitter: @matadorbooks

ISBN 9781 83859 152 6

British Library Cataloguing in Publication Data.
A catalogue record for this book is available from the British Library.

Printed and bound in the UK by T J International, Padstow, Cornwall
Typeset in 11pt Baskerville by Troubador Publishing Ltd, Leicester, UK

Matador is an imprint of Troubador Publishing Ltd

Thanks to my wife, Denise, daughters
Ama and Sable for their support.

To my sisters Nyoka, Claudette, Liz and Jean for their
suggestions, and to my brother, Hilton, for always
spotting the flaws that escape me.

To F Herbert for sound advice, as always.

introduction

This collection introduces, in SVG fiction, the first female private investigator, Cassie Providence.

contents

cassie providence

Some women I know began to fret when they hit the big three-O, but not me. 2014 pelt a kick where it hurt. For in that year Cassie Providence began to make her mark as a private detective. From that time, as one of the top three investigators in St Vincent and the Grenadines – SVG – when I took on your case, you could rely on my training in the police force. And, to be sure, if you look at a woman and only see shape and face, where will you find yourself but in peril?

Five-four, medium-build, I have a heart-shaped face and a headful of soft hair. The satin-black skin, rich eyebrows and almond-shaped eyes? I have to thank our Caribbean history for that. My friends don't think of me as tough, but they know I can defend myself. In the Thomas case that really set me on the way, two people got physical, and both had to crawl away. I was just climbing out of a steep crab hole when my career took off. A call deep into the night was how the whole thing began.

'Joel, the phone,' I grunted that dawn, nudging that 'vagabond' man of mine gently in the ribs. 'Go and check who.'

Night is for sleeping, didn't the blasted idiot provoking the house phone know that? Unless my father was critical, or my mother – even though the scoundrel ran off when I was seven

1

to search for oil in Trinidad – why would anyone call at that hour? I buried my face in the pillow, Joel might give in and answer.

But no luck. 'Vagabond' was in the land of dreams.

'Get the phone nuh,' I tried again. 'Darling. Sweetheart.'

'Leave it.' Joel rolled onto his back. 'It's probably a wrong number.'

'This time of the morning?'

'Zzzzzzz. Zzzzzzzz!'

'You just wait, see if I don't catch you.'

I sighed and rolled out of bed, snorting like a sour piglet. 'Ring off now,' I called out, 'stop now and it's me and you!'

'Mrs Providence? Cassie Providence?'

'Yes,' I mumbled.

'This is Mr Thomas.'

'Who?' I grumbled this time.

'Big-man Thomas.'

I knew Big-man Thomas. The whole of SVG knew him. There was a time when his smug grin could double the sales of the weekly papers, and tourists could sketch glasses to his eyes in their complimentary magazines. Shopkeeper turned businessman – he used to boast – he had spied a gap in the market, got a bank loan, and got to work.

After years abroad, Vincentians from England, Canada and the US flew back to the sun to thaw out, and to recapture those elements of their youth Nature still permitted. They handed over real Yankee dollars and crisp sterling for the fresh beef, stew pork, river fish, breadfruit, saltfish, mangoes and papaws locals took for granted. Big-man got to know a small fundraising group, and soon his van was eating up the mainland delivering day and night. The shop went, Big-man bought three houses to rent out and made his name and fortune. Business was slowing down now thanks to his gambling, which was on the up. Walk a mile in any direction, and you were bound to hear the rumours that he was in trouble with the bank.

I asked him, 'What you want, Big-man? Why you waking me up at this hour?'

'Sorry Mrs Providence,' he came back, 'but I have a problem.'

'What kind of problem?'

'My daughter Lynette, she didn't come home last night.'

'Why you telling me that?'

'You do a bit of detective work, don't you?'

'Yes,' I answered swiftly, no point telling him it was six weeks since my last proper case.

'A little bird chirped your name to me: it said you are an investigator.'

I switched on my brain, hoping he couldn't hear me rummaging on the table for paper and ink. 'Let me get my notebook.'

Of course I was an investigator! If I didn't believe in my work, what was I doing answering the phone at cock-crow?

'Give me the story, Big-man,' I said, notebook and pen now at hand. 'Start from the beginning.'

'Lynette is an assistant manager in a supermarket in Kingstown,' he explained after clearing his throat, 'she started as a cashier and worked her way up. No problems at home, and she's happy at work. But for some reason me and her mother can't figure out, she didn't make it home. My wife is on medication, you have to help us.'

He gave me Lynette's details – workplace, height, build, car registration, and her work number, his voice choking with emotion.

'What was she wearing,' I asked, when he finished the list. 'What kind of dress, what colour?'

'I don't study women's clothes, Providence,' Big-man mumbled, as if my question was below a true investigator.

'Don't you?' I said.

'No.'

'I thought you used to boast that you were the man for detail,' I pointed out. 'Didn't you go on TV bragging that if you boxed up lobster and plantains for a customer, you made sure the neighbour had mullets and bananas?'

'You just come by at eight, Providence,' he grumbled. 'I'm going to deliver tuna specials for some of my ex-pats, I should be back by then. If you find my daughter, I could put some serious business your way.'

He blew his nose, and I could hear the snivelling as if he was right next to me.

'Thanks, Big-man,' I said, 'you leave everything to me.'

When he rang off I stood there scratching my chin. If someone went missing in SVG it was usually because they wanted to bow out for a while. Pressure at work, an up-and-down relationship, liquor taking over, drugs eating away their brain, that kind of thing. I was intrigued but, best of all, I was happy. For Cassie Providence was on a case, and this one sounded big!

Even now, years later, when I take on a new case, I feel a tingle to go with the butterflies in my stomach. I can't wait to get going, but I have to fight off the feeling of danger round the next corner, or having to explain to my client that I had come to a dead end. In the police force we called this a 'five-dollar case', low priority, easy to suss in a small Caribbean country. But would I be able to solve it on my own?

That morning I couldn't go back to bed. Four o'clock is the sweetest time to sleep, but also the cruellest to be up. I sat at the window gazing at the Caribbean Sea. Silvery, placid, comforting. The same as the day before, and the one before that. Beautiful, heavenly, a scene to drive you to love. My gaze turned to the bed; 'Vagabond' was back in the land of dreams.

Flat on his back, peaceful, the hairs on his stomach and legs soft, I felt like jumping on him. The promise of a case made me feel hollow, anxious, 'Vagabond' had the arms to reassure me. But jump on him now, and he would put in a request for the same treatment every morning! So I hauled on a light white cotton dress and went downstairs to my tiny office to begin to plan.

I spent seven years in the SVG police force. I helped to settle family feuds, when they sent me to direct rush hour traffic in Kingstown in the midday sun, I didn't moan. Leeward, windward, the interior, the Grenadines, wherever they posted me, I was happy to let the residents have a taste of police justice. 'Mix and mingle', they taught us during training, gather what you can from every conversation; so, in every village or town, even when off duty, I never forgot that I was a policewoman.

Sergeant Stoute offered me his hand on my first day. 'Congratulations. Welcome to the force, constable Mulraine.'

'Thank you, sir.'

'But a word of advice. Act fair, do your duty, but don't go beyond. The hardened criminals who feel they are outside and above the law; the drug dealers and landowners who believe that *they* run the country with their dirty dollars; the rich lawyers who don't want to pay a dollar in taxes because they can recite a dozen Latin phrases and dress up in pretty gowns: those are the people to go after.'

Fresh from Police College, who was I to argue?

'Crime mostly takes care of itself in SVG,' Sergeant Stoute informed me, 'don't get overzealous during an investigation.'

'But sir,' I protested, 'we have to contact every witness to get a full picture so we can lock up the culprits in a case. You commit the crime, you must suffer in a dirty cell on bread and lime juice.'

'No.' Stoute patted me on the left shoulder and gave me the kind of reassuring smile I only got from my father. 'As police we must try not to upset the pattern, or magnify a fly into a lion. Girlfriend chasing boyfriend with a hoe on the way home from their plot of yams; neighbours pelting blows over ownership of a breadfruit tree; a jealous lover lacing a meal with turpentine: why turn a simple quarrel into a criminal offence?'

'You want us to teach Vincy people to reason, sir?'

'And to be reasonable. To lift themselves above a dispute; to sit down and talk instead of jumping up and down if you step on their toes.'

'I suppose I could try, sir.'

Stoute was tall, erect, handsome, with a proud blackness he carried everywhere. I followed his advice, but in my own way. I was my own woman, I had to play it the way I saw it. Those who came at me kicking and punching ended up on the floor, sometimes taking me with them. Bruise for bruise, you had to run with it, as they say. A youth on the way to a dance carrying a weapon went straight to jail, no ifs, no buts, if I was the officer who frisked him.

Van drivers made sure there were no dull days, some fool who could barely write his name was bound to come to the station and threaten the female officer who asked to see his licence. 'Ask your father who your mother was,' one idiot said to me, fingering his gold chain and blowing me a kiss. My colleague Neesha Crichton wanted to send him to hospital with a busted lip, but I watched him hard then got out the handcuffs. But no, I decided after a while, the crapaud wasn't worth the effort. 'Come back when you get to D in the alphabet,' I told him, cutting his licence into pieces with my scissors. 'And don't let the police catch you driving without your documents.'

We separated schoolgirls squabbling over a mobile phone, my body received so many blows I was sure forty would find me blue from head to toe. A woman rushing her fella in the street in a rage, lashing out with fist and handbag, would ignore the officer trying to keep the peace. I took home insults as well as bruises, but you wouldn't find me grumbling to my sergeant.

Down the Grenadines the fighting was mainly about land. Prominent people, 'the elite', they called themselves. These were the islands tourists came for, they told us at the station, their white sand was weightier than gold. And each man and woman seemed to want a parcel of this precious sand. I remember driving to prevent a brother choking his sister to death over breakfast in Bequia, 'Give me the deeds!' he was screeching when we got there. Another five minutes, and I'm sure we would have been dealing with a murder. And it was a murder in Kingstown that gave me a taste for detective work.

My sergeant had lined up a spell with the detective team, the officer leading the murder investigation was his cousin. It was mainly desk work to begin, and meeting after meeting to discuss progress. I listened, but didn't say much at first. I managed to ease my way in, and soon I was doing the door-to-door enquiries with Sylvia Peppy. When the team returned to the station empty-handed one rainy evening, I caught Inspector De Freitas trying to thump the life out of her desk.

I waited till she was alone, begged to join the team proper, and she agreed. Now we went out at night in teams of women or men, not mixed as before. We were lucky, for night is when people open up in a bar – to women if they could play the part, to men if they had the cash. After sponsoring drinkers beer and malt three nights in a row, each team came back with the same name. The confession came soon after, and without tears. I liked the feel of detective work, family disputes seemed petty now.

Some of the younger officers were after promotion, but Sergeant and Inspector didn't appeal to me. Longer spells with the detectives in town was what I was after, why chase stripes to weigh down my shoulders? One Friday deep into my service, the sergeant at Chateaubelair, Hilton Corea, called me into his office and shut the door behind me.

Corea was short and muscular, with a soft baby-face which was the brown shade of black our Caribbean history is always toying with. The talk was that he had joined up thinking the police force was one branch up from Scouts, but managed to disarm a knifeman on the journey home on his first day. He was brave and strong and liked action. Mention a fight, and he was flexing his staff and revving up his police motorbike to make an arrest.

'Mulraine,' Corea sang out my name that Friday, as though he was about to proposition me.

'Yes, sergeant,' I answered shyly, taking the chair opposite him he forgot to offer me.

'I have good news for you.'

I screwed up my face. One of his women had recently left him, and I knew he was putting the word about the station that he had a 'vacancy'.

'Yes sergeant?' I repeated, but this time adding a frown.

'I'm recommending you for a special unit for night operations. I think you're ready to move up.'

My hair started to itch, I was sure I could smell burning.

'Me sergeant?' I almost cried out.

'Yes Mulraine. Remember the six weeks you spent with the detective team in Kingstown?'

'Two months, sergeant.'

'No matter. Inspector De Freitas said you have the potential for detective work, and that Carib woman has a good police nose. It's time to start climbing the ladder.'

I wondered if he was confusing me with another Officer Mulraine in the leeward area. 'Thank you, sir,' I said, 'but when you said night work, you mean going after gangs deep into the mountains?'

Sergeant Corea took a sip of his cold beer. 'That's a possibility, yes.'

'And taking on the traffickers who live fast, and expect to perish round every blind corner?'

Another sip. 'With the elite squad you must be ready to use your training to the full, yes.'

'Then thank you but no, Sergeant Corea: the special unit not for Cassie Mulraine. I put in to train as a detective, what happened to my application?'

'I'll check.'

Five months later, when Corea showed me my name on his list again, I resigned on the spot. The mountain people crammed their three-score and ten years into twenty-two, I was happy to let my life flow the way our maker intended. My application to join the detective unit was sitting on some Inspector's desk, I wasn't going to take on the fast route like a female officer from Cedars. Besides, my cousin Spencer had promised to sponsor me, three years 'living in' with a wealthy Canadian family, and studying for a degree. And who wouldn't prefer that to sparring with the gangs who valued their life in the number of crocus bags of weed they could ship?

But good old Spencer. One evening not long after, I came home and found a message on my phone. The family he had lined up for me had moved to Nova Scotia.

'Sorry eh, Cassie. Truly sorry!'

I wasted a night on the phone to Ontario listening to his wife's feeble excuses. Spencer was on night shift, the madam explained, he would call me as soon as he got in. I knew he wouldn't phone, so I wasn't angry as I sat up waiting for his next promise. I wasn't angry, I was vex! I called Canada the next day, but now both husband and wife were working late.

'You damn coward, Spencer Sylvester!' I screamed down the phone. 'You just wait till you touch down in SVG. Guess who will be rolling out the red carpet!'

Out of a job, and with seven hundred dollars in my green bank book, it didn't take long for my little house in Reeves Level to turn into a shack. I wrote Spencer a three-page love letter, I cursed the foolish half of myself. How was I going to live? Where was I going to find money to run my car? Why didn't I ask for a transfer to traffic police, or look for another way out?

'Hand-to-hand fighting? I can handle that. Weapons? Now, that is worries.'

Officer Neesha Crichton from Mount Coke used to chant this daily as if it was the latest carnival road march. 'The night squad is promotion? No thank you!'

That was Neesha all over. When she got the invitation from Corea to track the dealers, she fed her boyfriend linseed with his tea, sea moss for breakfast and to wash down his dinner, and got herself pregnant. At least that was the rumour at the station. I couldn't go up that hill, but surely there was another way for a young female officer? Bang in the middle of this mad phase, I decided to become a private investigator.

The idea came to me one morning during my 'jailbird' breakfast. Yes, I was down to a small white loaf and black coffee by then. I was nibbling the bread when a voice whispered, 'Cassie, why don't you become a private detective? Sergeant Corea said you have the potential, why not give it a try?'

I couldn't sit at home forever. When you have nothing, you have to try something. So I took a van into Kingstown that afternoon, bounced into the police bar on Middle Street, and treated my former colleagues to beer with my last twenty dollars.

'What happen, Cassie, you just back from vacation?' Peter Lowpillow asked when I sponsored him a second *Hairoun* beer. 'You pick up a fat wallet on the streets of London?'

'I set up as a Private Investigator,' I told him and four officers, skipping out before they could ask when they could visit me at the asylum. 'Give out my number, spread the word.'

Before I left I 'borrowed' a camera and some binoculars from the police store. Then I called back a hundred dollars Neesha owed me and bought coloured pens, dark glasses, two old hats, a notebook and some scissors. If you drove by Reeves Level and saw a woman with fresh clothes in the porch looking out, good chance that woman was me. SVG was brimming with public insults, gossip, and innuendo, lawyers were raking in money for slander, some of the libel trade was bound to wash my way, wasn't it?

But not a figure from the road, not a brrrrrh! from the phone. Only the children on the way to or from school came near the house. For weeks, not a single inquiry.

I started to get up late, sometimes nine o'clock would find me in bed, my ears blocking out the malicious jabbering the radio announcers called debate. I would sit in the porch for an hour or so, then, when the sun began to sting, it was back to the bedroom feeling a waste of a woman. My clothes went sweaty and sour, my skin grey and flaky. My hair soon tangled up, dark lines grew on my nails when my purple nail varnish dried up. And then, out of the blue, a case!

'If I could find someone I would set him on Clayton. I'm sure he straying: he sprinkling on lotion, he never used to shave to go to work, but now he dressing in shirt and tie! Some Jezebel feeding him like the "fatted calf", his thighs can't fit into his trousers.'

In typical Vincy fashion, a woman from Rose Hall was discussing her husband with a friend in Lizzies Restaurant in Kingstown. The woman had a wide flat face with a small triangular nose dead in the middle, purple lipstick, and thick hair poking out the sides of her blue headtie. Her square polka dot dress was feeling the strain.

'Cassie Mulraine, Miss.'

'What?' The woman gave me a 'bad eye', as if I was trying to sell her stale fish from the boot of an old car.

I dragged my chair over to their table. 'I'm an investigator.'

She gave her eyes licence over the bits of my body the chair didn't hide. 'You?' she said. 'You sure?'

I got up so she could take in the full me. 'Yes. I used to be a police detective, but now I have my own agency.'

She looked as if she might want fish after all. 'Where you based?'

'Right here in town.' I kept the reply vague to buy time.

'Where exactly?'

I turned to go back to my table, 'breaking old style' as Vincies say, so she wouldn't guess that I needed her as much as she needed me. 'You want your husband exposed or not?'

'How much you charge?'

'For a basic *WARB*, two hundred dollars a day,' I said, because no one believes you are a professional if they could understand your language.

'What's that?'

'*Watch And Report Back*,' I came back quickly, so she wouldn't know I had just made it up.

'Watch the scoundrel for a week, then,' she said after giving me her husband's description and other essentials.

'Every place he visit, write it down. And get the Jezebel's name so I can fix both of them good and proper.'

She counted out a healthy mix of twenties and tens, and I hurried out the restaurant before her friend could ask her to reconsider. A case, money! It didn't seem real.

How does a PI prepare for her first big case? List names of people to see, places to visit, and plan her moves? I don't know about others, but I went and did my hair at a salon in Belvedere. Had it shampooed and plaited into a proud cylinder at the back of my head like Queen Nefertiti. Do my nails as well, I said to the male assistant at the salon, and thin out the eyebrows.

Two hours later, I was off to Pembroke to collect my 'uniform' – a lilac blouse and charcoal trousers from a seamstress who knew how to dress a Caribbean woman. Before I went to bed I took a long shower, then creamed my face and cocoa-buttered my legs. After months cooped up like Mother Hen, I was ready for the world again.

The next day I tracked the husband along the narrow streets of the capital. Hiding behind a newspaper, or ducking round concrete pillars, no police uniform to protect me, Kingstown seemed a different place now. I was on my own, feeling my way as an investigator. I ate warm restaurant food on expenses, every woman Clayton joked with in the queue at the post office ended up in my book. When he flirted with an old flame at the market, I took a snap then got her name from the vendor.

Monday, Tuesday, Wednesday, I trailed the land-tax officer as he went about his work and play. But tracking is never enough – I learned that lesson early. When you can't find dirt at home you have to dig or scratch at work. So I slipped one of his co-workers, Selma Chester, two twenty-dollar bills and asked her about their team.

'They give us a bonus six weeks ago,' Selma explained, 'my husband wanted a new fridge, but the extra could only keep the family in flour, oil, soap and sardines for a month.'

'And Clayton?'

'Clayton change.' Selma seemed happy for her colleague. 'He looking double healthy these days, something definitely agreeing with him. He spending cash like Christmas and Easter fall on his birthday.'

Clayton was solid, with a full face, a heavy mouth and fat cheeks. A thin moustache was probably there in case the lotion didn't work its magic. Remove the moustache, I thought as he queued at a snackette for an orange juice and a bag of crush-cakes, and he would resemble a happy pig halfway through a bunch of boiled bananas.

He had me trekking to Seaside Restaurant, Jessop's Snack Bar, Franherbert Inn, large plate, large juice, at each eating place. Then, on Thursday, a change! Carrying a large ping-wing basket, he caught a van to Indian Bay at eleven. Got him, I said to myself, my first victim!

From the shade of a tree twenty yards away, I could see him changing into blue swimming trunks. When he had squeezed as much flesh as would agree into the bathing suit, he flexed his arms like a man limbering up for a serious romantic workout. He was waiting for a woman, I was ready to bet one of his wife's twenty-dollar bills, wasn't Indian Bay a perfect spot for lovers?

The man at the end of my binoculars opened the basket, and took out a loaf and a tin of corned beef. Soon he was filling his mouth, looking up at the main road every now and again like a man expecting company. He was in a hurry, if his lover had an appetite she would have a job catching up.

Five minutes passed, another five, and a further set. A woman joined him just as he was unwrapping a beef roti. I put her at thirty, good-looking, with a wide sexy smile. No wonder his wife was worried!

Click, I got her face, click, I added her profile – snap first, get name later. Back to the binoculars, I saw Clayton pointing to a spot on the beach. Was she going to swim before the afternoon frolic? The woman set off along the hot black sand away from the vendors. Aha, I could see it now: she was going to get ready, they had a hideout behind the rocks on the far side of the beach!

When Clayton got up and began to tiptoe away, I knew I was really earning that deposit in *Lizzies*. They were going to play in the sea then 'cool off' together where the boys and girls skipping afternoon school wouldn't interrupt them. But now my binoculars couldn't pick out the woman. I switched back just in time to catch Clayton plunging into the sea with a loud splash.

It was boiling. I had tracked him for a week, the woman was gone, or was struggling into her swimsuit. Why not join Clayton in the water and see what he had to say for himself?

He didn't just bring his basket, he was prepared for a dip. I was still green as a PI, a change of clothes meant a journey back home. So, in a fraying brown bra and yellow panty, I crawled into the sea close to where he was swimming. I dived, then came up for breath. And again, until I was about five metres away.

'The water sweet, not true?' I called out to Clayton, splashing it over my body.

He turned to his right and gazed at me. He looked terrified. He began to paddle and run and splash back to land like a swimmer spotting a mermaid. I saw him stuff his things into the basket, by the time I got my clothes on he was hailing a van back to town.

'You have a good man there,' I told his wife as I collected my fee in the restaurant on the Friday. 'You can trust him with your little sister.'

After that, the news trickled out that I was a PI, and jobs began to drift in. Not top-quality stuff, but work all the same. Strangers would nudge me in the street and pass me a hundred to record what their partner had for lunch and who paid. Or a businessman would slip me an envelope to guard his property overnight, with a welcome bonus if things were quiet.

Big-man lived in Cane Garden. From the veranda you could catch Kingstown on your right, compact and so beautiful it almost hurt your eyes. To the left was Arnos Vale Airport, quiet, waiting for the next LIAT from Barbados or St Lucia to wake things up. Thanks to his 'ex-pats', Big-man had a view most of them could never afford.

He was a short man, and well on the way to round. 'A quarter of everything,' he called himself – African, East Indian, Carib, European. Fifty-three, with wavy hair and smooth black skin, he looked healthy and shiny. Before we got down to business I expected a tour of his palace, and I wasn't wrong: no Vincy would let a visitor get away that easy. Nine pictures of Lynette looked down at me, each one with a pretty smile. Why would a beautiful and happy daughter suddenly disappear? After the show we sat in the cool of the veranda and Big-man's wife, Girlin, brought us two glasses of guava juice, and reminded him to collect the rent from one of their tenants.

'Sorry I woke you up at dawn, Mrs Providence,' Big-man apologised, rubbing his puffy eyes. 'When Girlin told me Lynette wasn't home, and her phone would just ring and ring and then switch off, I nearly went crazy.'

'She ever slept out before?'

'She isn't that kind of girl.'

'What kind of girl is she then?'

'Just your usual twenty-two-year old.'

'Who can't find her way home from Kingstown to Cane Garden? Who forgets to phone, and whose mobile is on and off like a light switch?'

'That isn't my Lynette. She doesn't want for anything. My girl would never do a deed to hurt me and her mother. We help her with her car, we give her $300 spending money every month, someone must have drugged her or kidnapped her or something.'

'You informed the police?' I asked.

'Police?' Big-man looked at me as if I was trying to persuade him to swim from St Vincent to Tobago. 'Them jokers? Those clowns who couldn't find a raindrop in a storm?'

'Put in a report,' I said, for it irritated me when people knocked the force. 'Call headquarters.'

'I don't want the police involved,' he grumbled. 'Too risky. I want *you* on the case.'

'Did you contact Lynette's work?'

'Yes. I called her boss, Trotman said she seemed fine.'

'Friends?'

'I only know two, Beverley Hinds and Patsy Brown from school and work. I already spoke to them, they don't know where she is.'

'Give me the numbers,' I said, 'let me have a try.'

He had the three numbers on a slip of paper. As I was scribbling them down his mobile rang. He glanced at it but didn't answer. A minute later, it went again. He cut it off this time, but not before I could glimpse the surname, Veluto.

'Boyfriend?' I asked as he fumbled with the mobile.

'Lynette isn't into those things.'

'How old did you say she was, twenty-two?' I asked.

Big-man couldn't see where I was aiming.

'Yes,' he answered.

'Does that make her a girl or a young woman?'

'Mrs Providence, you just find my daughter!' Big-man quietly exploded. 'Three hundred dollars to start, plus expenses. Just bring her home.'

He had his hand out ready to shake when his wife brought the house phone.

'Some man with a funny name,' she said.

'Excuse me.' Big-man grabbed the phone and ducked into the nearest room on the left. I felt flat. Had to be someone reporting that he had found Lynette, the case was over before I even got started. But a minute later Big-man came out and said, 'One of my clients, Mrs Providence. Call me later and let me know how you're getting on.' I finished my drink, raced into my Toyota and drove off. Three names in my notebook weren't much to go on, but for three hundred I would have driven from Fancy to Fitz-Hughes and back at midnight.

My mind told me to start in Kingstown, so I drove to Bay Street. If you snatched someone, or if you wanted to hide away, where better to head than for one of the Grenadine islands on an early boat out?

The wharf was quiet for a Saturday. For those Vincies who fancied white beaches instead of black sand for a day, the ferries were nodding and waiting patiently. I sat in the car and put the binoculars on the passengers. Did I truly expect to see Lynette Thomas? No, my instinct told me she was still on the mainland. But I kept watching anyway: who could ever get tired of the blend of people we have in St Vincent and the Grenadines? When the ferries were specks in the distance, I put away the camera and binoculars.

The airport was next on my plan, four miles away, fifteen minutes with the traffic in your favour. But I decided to try Lynette's friends first. Beverly's phone was engaged so I phoned Patsy Brown.

I could almost hear her sigh, but I couldn't miss her sucking her teeth.

'I don't know who you are, Miss,' she grunted before I could give my name. 'But I have my washing and cooking and ironing to do. Don't bother me, you hear.'

'And a good morning to you,' I said.

Saturday overseas might be busy, but in SVG it is like a rest day for most businesses. After two o'clock when the supermarkets close, Kingstown resembles a ghost town. I called Lynette's boss at home, hopefully, he would have better manners. Lynette left work on Friday tired but sparky, Veffrey Trotman was happy to talk to me, she drove off with a man. He saw them through the office window.

Surely this couldn't be the daughter Big-man described.

'Who?' I asked.

'I don't know, never seen the guy before.'

'Her fella?'

'I don't monitor her love life. She is a hardworking deputy, good with the accounts, that's all I care about.'

'Who was driving?' I asked.

'The man, I think.'

'Whose car, Lynette's?'

'No. She said she came to work by van this morning.'

'Thanks.'

The airport didn't give up much. The taxi people knew the Thomas family, the airline clerks and porters too. Lynette didn't come near the ET Joshua terminal, they were all positive, I was wasting my time there. I decided to take an early lunch.

As I was sinking a large glass of linseed in a snackette, it hit me that I was like a woman trying to make bread with sand. Big-man Thomas was definitely hiding something, he was playing me. His twenty-two-year old was still a 'girl', no money worries, she was the perfect Vincy daughter. So perfect that Lynette could go off with a man, probably spend the night with him, and forget to phone home and lie that she was staying overnight with Beverly or Patsy. What was Big-man hiding from, why didn't he want to report that Lynette was missing to the police?

And who was the man she drove off with? Where did they go, where was her car, and where were they now? Did Big-man know she had more than female friends?

I phoned Beverley Hinds a second time. I was Lynette's elderly aunt Rhonda, I told her in my best granny voice, I didn't drive, Lynette was supposed to take me food-shopping, but she didn't turn up. I couldn't get through to her mother – my sister – and Lynette's phone was off. Did something upset her at work?

'No. Friday was busy, Lynette was in the middle of the action as always.'

'And no one left the premises threatening this and that?'

'Not that I know.'

'Why isn't she answering her phone then?'

'That doesn't sound like Lynette, you can't separate her from her metal twin.'

'Who's on the other end?'

'Someone with hearing like a bat – she's always whispering.'

'Boyfriend? Man-friend?'

'Could be. She's friendly with some fella.'

'Who?'

'I only glimpsed him once. I think he's English, or something like that.'

'English-English?'

'No. Vincy-English?'

'And she hasn't introduced him?'

'No. But the way she talks about him, you would think they're already married.'

'What's his name?'

'Wray – with a W, like the Jamaican rum.'

'Where does he live?'

'I can't tell you that.'

In Vincy talk this meant she didn't know, not that she was holding on to some secret.

'Thanks still,' I said.

After this it was back to Kingstown. Back to Tokyo watching the vans and listening to the conversations, then to the police station to see what I could hear. It was a quiet day, the police were playing cards, dominoes and draughts, and swapping stories about the latest crimes. No Lynette, not a single Thomas, came up.

When I got home I transferred the questions in my notebook to the whiteboard in my office: Where was Lynette's car? If Wray was the man who picked her up from work, where did they spend the night? And if it wasn't him, who else was on her scene? Even if she ran a tangled love life, why not let her parents know she was safe?

Big-man was on the phone before I could wonder what was for supper.

'You found her yet?' he gushed like a dog slobbering at a bone. 'You put the word out among your contacts?'

'Mr Thomas,' I told him straight, 'I can't find your daughter when you don't want to tell me anything.'

'Anything like what?'

'If she has a boyfriend, where she goes after work. The reason she might want to leave you dangling.'

'That's *your* job, Providence, that's for you and your contacts to find out. You're the investigator, not true?'

'Yes. And you're the one hiding the information that could trace her.'

'You don't want the case then?' Big-man Thomas growled.

'Not if you're going to hold back the facts from me.'

'I'm paying you, Providence, you're not working for fresh air. I earn my money, you know, I don't just pluck it off a plum tree like some people believe.'

After four years in the force, Corporal Marcella Culzac from Cumberland introduced me to big-time gambling. Fountain, Basin Hole, Orange Hill, Rose Hall, Chateaubelair, Spring, a sniff of a money-pot, and we buzzed in like honey bees: police, musicians, teachers, doctors, farmers, businesswomen, even a LIAT captain. In the basement of a shop, or cooped up in a shed away from the house, ten to fifteen of us played cards and dominoes for twenty dollars a game, more when the going was sweet, or when it was pay day.

One evening in Georgetown my luck was in. 'Flushes' and 'Straights' like peas in *rummy*, I was on top form. The dominoes were fizzing in my hands, I could have played in a blindfold. I bought drinks for my police crew and still had a pile to carry home. The Sunday morning I woke up with an almighty headache. But that was only the half of it. When I finally got my eyes open, I found a man standing over me. Headache or no headache, I shot up from the bed.

'What you doing in my house?'

The man was about five-nine, with sleepy-looking eyes and thin arms. He wasn't bad looking, but this wasn't the time for that.

'What you doing here?' I repeated when he didn't answer.

'Looking after you,' he said, as if he was a doctor. 'You're lucky I'm not some vagabond.'

His voice was soft, melodic, and when I could focus properly, I recognised him as a member of the gambling posse. A trumpeter in the police band, he had a hard face, yet gentle and caring. He held up a large wad of tens and twenties as if he was my lucky charm. I could remember winning big, but no point in asking him how much. He placed the money on the table and sat on the edge of the bed.

Cassie girl, I said to myself, this can't go on, it has to stop. You're too old to wake up like this on a Sunday morning. Make Saturday your last wild night.

All the while 'Vagabond' sat there quietly watching me as if we woke up together every Sunday morning like man and wife. My hair a wild mess, my clothes smoky and sweaty, my body was calling out for soap and water.

'Fixed you a coffee,' he said.

'I need to shower first,' I explained.

'Then go ahead,' he replied. 'Don't let me stop you.'

'I only have on my underwear.'

'Go ahead,' he repeated softly, 'I don't mind.'

I don't know why, but I felt comfortable with him. He didn't threaten, he didn't make me feel self-conscious. Any other man and I would have been ordering him out of my house or screaming blue murder. But not 'Vagabond': it was all in his eyes, the way he seemed at ease, protective.

'Well, don't say I didn't warn you,' I said.

I'm average height for Caribbean women, I didn't have a problem with the giants who believe long legs are a woman's greatest gift. I'm happy with my body, the police force taught me to be comfortable with who I am. A birthmark just above my left knee used to make me feel awkward and uneasy, but I barely notice it now. So, sliding out the bed, I grabbed a towel and aimed for the shower.

'Vagabond' didn't react. Was he that cool, or just playing cool? He wasn't afraid of women, it was obvious. And I liked that.

'Don't forget the coffee waiting,' he said, and I could hear a dip in his voice for the first time. 'Best to take it hot!'

Luck came to me early. Again and again, in case after case, just when I was running out of ideas, Lacy Luck would give me a gentle nudge. And she was with me the Sunday after I took the Lynette Thomas case.

That morning, me and Joel drove to Rawacou for our weekly relax. Some returnees were having a picnic when we got there. Between fifteen and twenty men and women working in their quiet, efficient, overseas way. Joel made straight for the pool, but I liked to cool off before dipping my feet. I was strolling along the beach when I met a woman picking up pretty pebbles.

'Hot today, isn't it?' she said, dropping the pebbles carefully into a little blue purse.

She had a low delightful voice, careful on each word.

'English?' I said, hoping she wasn't the sensitive type.

She gave me a smile. 'Vincentian,' she answered. 'But yes, I used to live in England.'

'Enjoying it back home?' I asked.

'You can't beat the West Indies. Me and my son have been all over mainland SVG. Wray is going to book us a tour to the Grenadines for my birthday.'

You could make up names for your child, but slim chance two people would land on the same one just like that.

'Wray?' I said.

'Yes, Wray. With a W.'

'Wray Fife?'

'Why, do you know him?'

'He's a friend of my cousin,' I said.

'Well next time you see him, remind him to phone if he's staying out. It's a sin to waste food like that.'

'I'll give him your message.'

'I suppose he's still hanging out at the old banana-boxing station in Belmont?'

24

'Yes,' I said, thankful for the lead. 'That's where I saw him last.'

'Then let him know his mother is still alive. He might be twenty-five, but he's still my son.'

'I will,' I promised.

She gave me her number, and I watched her amble back to her group with her precious pebbles. When she was out of sight I rushed to the pond where Joel was cutting the water like a shark.

'Change of plan,' I shouted above the crashing of the waves. 'Work.'

We took the shortcut through Calder, and turned left at the Mespo road. Up, then down, then round, and round again, and we were in Belmont.

An old tractor, younger sister to a rotting wooden bus, was rotting near the entrance to the banana station. Joel parked by the road. I got out, if anyone tried to run off in that direction, they would run right into his arms.

I brushed aside the tall razor grass stalks that liked to leave their mark on your legs. A dozen more ginger steps, and I was by the boxing plant. At the side of the building ten youngsters – five boys, five girls – were sitting in a circle like students at Bible Study. When they saw me ten became two before I could get a good look. The youths skipped through the river and dived into a banana field. Not Bible Study then.

'Why your friends took off like that?' I asked the two left.

The stays looked at each other, then shrugged me their reply.

'Lynette and Wray were in the mix?'

They looked me over slowly. Their verdict? They didn't say. Something in the banana field was calling them too.

I pushed the heavy wooden front door with my right foot and stepped into the building. Huge place, hot, with the oily smell of drying copra. But not too big to notice a photograph of Lynette on a window ledge. She was close by, I could tell. If not here, then hiding with one of the banana fielders.

The back of a monster American fridge almost blocked the door to a room on the right. I pulled in my stomach till I could squeeze in sideways. My hand went straight to my mouth. For right behind the door was a mountain of yellow and green coconuts, boxes of ginger, crocus bags of green soursops, yellow plums, mangoes, zabuca, and at least ten crates of ground provision.

Had to be more, I was thinking, and there was. In the freezer I found lobsters, crayfish, conchs, tuna and eels, the delicacies Big-man sold to his customers. Were the Bible Study crew one of Big-man's suppliers? As I was about to shut the freezer door, someone grabbed me by the throat.

'What are you doing here?'

Screaming when someone attacks you wastes energy and time, you hand the attacker all the shots. Better to get some idea of his strength and work out his grip. Picture the attacker, Cassie, I told myself, plan your moves. Think him, wait for things to level out. But it wasn't easy when his left hand blocked my throat, and his right hand jammed mine so hard into my back that my eyes began to water.

He eased the hold on my throat a little to allow me to reply. 'Well?'

I didn't answer. Didn't make a sound, even though my right shoulder felt like a fire was blazing in it.

The man was strong. Firm grip, solid biceps. Our training prepared us for all types, but this one was tall; I would have to get him low, and work with that. The perfume on him, and the hot breath on the back of my head? Forget some woman's darling, I told myself, keep your focus, shut out the hurt.

'What's your name, what are you looking for?'

Still no reply from me. The fire in my right shoulder was

spreading down my arm, I was sure my muscles were going to melt off the bone. I bit into my lips hard to even out the pain – top lip, bottom lip, bottom lip, top lip. The attacker upped the pressure on my throat. I closed my eyes and tried to picture a rainy night to take my mind off the strength of his fingers.

'What are you doing here?'

Pain, but I let my slow, dull breathing do the talking for me. This confused him, I could tell. As he was thinking of what to do or ask next, I relaxed the muscles in my throat for a fraction of a second to allow a draw of air into my windpipe. Now! I jerked my head back towards him – and away from his grip. At the same time I kicked his right ankle and forced his right leg out like half a ladder.

He lost his balance, and his hand came away from my throat. Now! Now! I backed my left elbow hard into his stomach, once, twice, then once more. He grunted and doubled up. My right hand now free, I grabbed him by the neck and hurled him over my right shoulder. Flat on his back, Wray Fife, the image of his mother.

'You stay right there,' I said, as he tried to get up. 'Don't move, or my husband will join us and spoil the fun.'

I waited for my shoulder to cool then I nodded to Wray. He bounced to his feet as if he was teaching me an exercise move to firm up my thighs.

'Where's Lynette?' I asked.

'I don't know,' he mumbled.

'Where is she, Wray?'

'I don't know, I haven't seen her since Thursday.'

'What time?'

'After four.'

'You tried her mobile?'

'Yes, but there's no answer. I'm really worried about her.'

'You two have a relationship?'

He rubbed his right lobe gently, he seemed the protective type.

'All the goods in here,' I said, 'the youngsters supplying Big-man?'

'I don't know.'

'And you have no idea where Lynette is?'

'No.'

'You don't seem to know much,' I said. 'Your mother said you could give a geography lesson on SVG.'

'My mother doesn't know anything,' he sneered. 'She thinks I'm going back to England, but like hell. I'm setting up my own business right here in SVG. Tell her that when you see her next.'

'No, *you* tell her.' I stretched out my right hand. 'Pass me your mobile.'

I scrolled through the *Contacts* then returned it.

'Say hello to Lynette for me,' I said.

He snatched the phone, then, a few minutes later, he too was skipping across the river.

Me and Joel drove through the narrow streets of Belmont, but no sign of Lynette's car, and the youngsters all seemed to be indoors. On the way home I got Joel to phone Lynette's number. She didn't pick up. He phoned again, still no answer. Leave a message, I said to him, pretend you're an admirer.

'Hi sexy.' Joel dug up a deep husky voice I hoped he would never try on me. 'Give me a call, my little precious, I'm missing you so bad. I can't get through another night without those tender arms.'

Ten minutes later the mobile rang.

'Who's this?' Lynette asked, her voice breathless with excitement.

'Cassie Providence,' I whispered.

She cut off the line, and off it stayed.

The Thomas family rented three houses. I remembered the

newspaper article saying that the wife was in charge of them, but the paper didn't say where they were. That afternoon I dropped Joel home, then watched the Thomas house for the third time. I remembered the wife saying something about the rent, who did the collecting?

Just after two Mrs Thomas left home and drove to a house in Prospect. She was there for about fifteen minutes. A thin woman, with sickly sketched on her face, my binoculars picked her out returning to her car with a slow walk, as if her stick-legs were columns of lead. I waited for her to drive off then knocked at the door. The tenant was a dread in his forties in a green vest, his short locks grey and tatty.

'Yes, Miss,' he said, 'what you after?'

'The lady who was just here, she didn't look happy.'

'Mrs Thomas?'

'Yes.'

'Just a little family problem, she said. She's a nice lady.'

'Nice how?'

'Understanding. I could only pay half-rent, she took that and said to give her the rest next month. Thank goodness it's not her husband or her daughter, those two always screaming for their money, no good telling them my yam sales were down. The daughter especially. She's always right up in your face, $10 a week interest adding if you're late with a payment. She slapped my daughter one Sunday, and threatened to box her down the gulley: she was lucky my wife was home that morning, otherwise I wouldn't be here talking to you.'

Later that evening Joel fixed dinner, then we went to the back of the house to enjoy the cooling sea breeze in the hammocks he built when we moved in. The events of the day tying up my head, Joel set up his tenor steelpan and began to play. A soft and beautiful tune, and a little sad. In no time I was asleep.

Outside of his work Joel, Sergeant Stoute, Constable Grafton

King and Corporal Werrican Bushay had a police 'combo' that played at weddings or socials. That Monday they had a booking for a new doctor, Noval Punnett, just back from Cuba, and I went along. Over seventy guests were there to welcome home the latest medic – family, friends, well-wishers, the inevitable smiling politicians. The music was mellow, the food and drink a real hit. And, best of all, Lacy Luck had slipped in with me.

As I was at the front of the hall enjoying the music, she touched me on the right shoulder. I turned round and got a surprise. For who was there mingling with the crowd? Big-man Thomas himself, in a crisp white shirt. No concerned-father look, just a man enjoying a beer and chunky fried chicken. Thank you, Lacy Luck, I said out loud. And thank you 'Vagabond'.

I put on my dark glasses, and a tatty granny hat I always store in the car. I kept my head down, watching Big-man closely, but keeping out of sight. During the interval he went to the kitchen for more breast and, through the half-open door, I heard him whispering to a man with two pens in his shirt pocket.

'What happen, Mr V,' Big-man sounded like a farmer handed a saucer of banana fritters for his dinner after a hard day in the fields. 'You didn't run the story on Friday.'

'It was too late, man.'

'One hundred percent it will be out this week?'

'Front page news. With a beautiful colour picture of Lynette under the headline, KIDNAPPED.'

'Thanks, Mr Ed.' Big-man could see a large plate of stewed pork and tender dasheen following the fritters. 'If things go to plan I'll sponsor the family a UK holiday. They apply a fresh layer of paint on Buckingham Palace just so Crisco Veluto could take a picture.'

At last I could cut through the Soufriere volcano mist. Lynette's disappearance; Big-man hiring me for the case; his refusing to take the call next to me; the goods at Belmont; the conversation with the newspaper editor: the mist was clearing, the picture was forming in my mind. But just as you can't make bread with mango, I couldn't strike without evidence.

Next day, after another drive through Belmont, I sat in a hot car watching the store again. Out with the glamour of the PI, in with a large dose of patience. No visitors, no sign of Lynette or Wray. A Honda parked by the door was the only change from the previous day. Still no Lynette at work, no ransom request, where was she?

The building was locked, but I suspected they were in there. Just after seven, dusk coming on, I phoned Joel and told him I might be late.

'What time to expect you?' he asked, and I couldn't miss the longing in his voice.

'I don't know.'

'Wait up?'

'Yes,' I begged. 'Stay.'

As I was putting away my mobile a vehicle belted past me. Scattering stones and dirt, the driver was clearly in a hurry. I knew this part of the country well, so I followed with my headlights off.

Once it hit the main road the car eased up. At the roundabout in Arnos Vale it turned left. Calliaqua, Brighton, Diamond, I followed it to Kingshill. A man climbed out the car. He entered a house and, a moment later, a light clicked on downstairs. I waited, then tiptoed in the dark to the house. The front door was ajar, I thanked the man and eased in sideways.

It was one of those places with the porch level with the road, and the kitchen, bathroom and dining room downstairs. Curious design, but popular. I sat in the darkness of the porch and listened.

'Drop me off and wait,' a female voice said. 'Park at the end of the road and I'll walk from there.'

'Suppose your mother sees you?'

'I'll use the door downstairs.'

'What about the neighbours?'

'Forget them, they're old people, they go bed early.'

'Everything's under control?'

'Better be.'

'What does he want to see you about?'

'He didn't say. Probably something to do with the offer.'

'He could have told you over the phone!'

'Big-man likes to play things careful, you never know who might be listening.'

The light clicked off, so I scrambled back to the car. Back to another hot night on the road, Big-man wasn't the only one who earned his money.

Thanks to the traffic I didn't have to get close to the Honda now. At the top of Sion Hill, the car took a left for Cane Garden. I parked at the end of the road. Not for long, and not far from Wray. Lynette sneaking home in the dark made me scratch my chin, but I had enough meat to add to the bones Big-man Thomas fed me. At last, I could make a proper soup.

Mercifully, the final journey of the night was short. Frenches, two miles from Cane Garden was where it ended. The car took a right off the main road and pulled up at a bungalow. I waited until the two silhouettes were inside then phoned Big-man Thomas with the address and directions.

'Bring 8 000 dollars,' I said, not giving him a chance to ask how, why or maybe. 'Ransom to pay the kidnappers.'

I slumped under the steering wheel feeling hot, sweaty, and totally drained. Police work was hard, life as a PI was even tougher. But no point sitting there feeling sorry for myself, there was still work to do. I dragged myself from the car, stepped over the culvert, and rapped on the door.

Lynette opened it, and stood on the mat staring at me with

a sour look. She was thin but full, and she didn't let her white merino dim her figure. Her thinness made her seem tall, but we met eye to eye. The small, wild, wide-apart eyes gave her a strikingly beautiful look, she could outdo all her photographs at the Thomas palace. I wasn't expecting a 'Good Evening', so when she lifted the merino and slowly did up the buttons of her jeans I took that as my welcome instead.

'Lynette Thomas,' I said softly, stepping inside the perfume-scented room. 'The young lady the family has been praying for in church twice a day.'

'I don't know why,' she said, closing the door behind me and staying close.

'No?'

'No.'

'I think you do.'

'You can think what you like,' she said. 'Anyway, what are *you* doing here?'

I took in the room – small, comfortable, with a wardrobe, settee, table, probably one they rented. A mobile on the table was playing soul.

'*Me?*' I said. 'Do you know me?'

'Of course I do, you're the woman who got some man to phone me: Cassie Providence.'

'How do you know that?'

She couldn't come up with an answer, so Wray came to her rescue from the settee.

'I told her,' he said. 'I told her you were looking for her.'

Lynette gave him a hard stare. 'You keep out of it, Wray,' she ordered him. 'Don't say or do anything, let me handle things.'

Wray scratched his chin and forced a smile. No doubt about who was running things.

I asked, 'Where was your hideout? This house or the one in Kingshill?'

Lynette kissed her teeth. 'I wasn't hiding anywhere.'

'Your parents and your manager have been searching everywhere for you, where were you then?'

'It was just a misunderstanding.'

She went and sat on Wray's lap.

'What was?' I asked.

She began to play with his hair, combing it with her fingers, curling, inhaling it. 'The whole thing.'

'Your plan isn't going to work, is it?' I said.

'What plan?'

'You and Wray setting up together,' I said.

She gave a hollow laugh. 'Who told you that nonsense?'

'Stealing your father's customers is nonsense, is it?'

'I don't know where you got that idea.' Lynette was still laughing. 'But if that's the best you can come up with, you need to go back to investigator school.'

'Who told you I was an investigator?' I said.

She eased herself up from Wray's lap, and waltzed over to where I was standing. She came right up into my face. I could smell her perfume, and the rawness of a twenty-two-year old woman.

'Cassie,' she snarled, 'I'm not afraid of you, you know.'

I inched closer to her, so close that our noses were almost touching.

'It's Mrs Providence to you, not Cassie.'

She didn't like this. Her nostrils flared, her eyes turned wild. We stood in the middle of the room, like lovers building up to a tender kiss. Then suddenly, Thwack! Thwack! And another. Thwack! My ears began to ring, stars floated across my eyes. The slaps took me by surprise, but I knew what to do. I turned my head and offered her the other cheek.

'Here,' I said. 'Try this one.'

Lynette made a fist on her right hand. Firm, tough. I was

going to pay for interrupting them, I was going to regret I was born with a mouth. She gave me a sweet smile. Should I return the compliment? No. Better to watch this woman closely, to see what was behind the grin now replacing the smile.

She broke the fist, and it took me a while to figure out why. It was because she had a better idea – a backhand slap instead of a punch. I kept my eyes on her, not a single blink. Slap number four, a punch, a kick, I had to be ready for it.

Lynette eased herself away from me and stepped back two paces. I waited. I could hear a moth serenading the light bulb, and a dog yelping outside the window. Then, just when I thought her tank was low, Lynette's right arm dipped below her left hip, and she began to swing. Every sense in my body on 'High', I saw the arm rising, but in slowed down slow-motion.

Up came the arm. There, a bit higher, higher still. Here at last. I was ready. I trapped her wrist and squeezed it hard. It felt soft and tender, but I didn't ease up the pressure. Burn, squeeze, burn. Squeeze, burn, squeeze, burn. I saw the prettiness drain from Lynette's face. She began to kick, and lashed out with her left hand – wild blows, but they hurt just the same.

I stopped the burning, gripped her fingers, and squeezed them together. She swung with her left hand, and connected with my forehead. My head jerked back but I kept my grip. Now, one by one, I separated her fingers. Then I bent her middle finger back as far as it could go.

'Aaaahhhhhhhh,' she screamed. 'Let me go, you dry-up bitch!'

Wray sprang up, it was two against one now. He grabbed Lynette by the waist and tried to pull her away. But she had her left hand locked round my neck, clinging to me like a child afraid of a tall stranger. He pulled, she wouldn't let go. So he slipped his hands between us and shoved us apart.

'Stay out of it Wray,' Lynette shrieked, 'leave the bitch to me!'

In no time she bounced back at me and began to kick

out. But wilder now, catching me on the shin and the knees, anywhere that would accept a blow. Fist after fist came my way, I ducked, shifted my body left and right to escape them. Kicks too, Lynette was mad. I caught one leg, then the other, and crossed them at the ankle. She lost her balance and landed on her backside on the floor.

'You wait, you little bitch,' she hollered. 'I'll get you, you'll see. One dark night when you're out somewhere, I'll kick you so hard no baby will ever come out of you!'

She pushed herself up, and crawled back to Wray's lap, leaving me standing there horrified. As he was trying to calm her the front door opened and Big-man Thomas barged in.

'What-what-what's going on?' Big-man shrieked and stammered at the same time.

Lynette shot up. She separated herself from Wray and fixed her clothes like a woman with three hands. Big-man took in the scene for a while then rushed over to her. He put an arm on her shoulder and made to hug her. Lynette tensed, like a girl who has grown up and no longer wants her father's hand to cross a busy road.

'Lynette, thank goodness you're safe,' Big-man slobbered. 'Me and your mother couldn't sleep at night, what happened? Who kidnapped you? Where did they have you tied up?'

'Big-man,' I interrupted, taking a chair at the table, 'you can skip all that foolishness now.'

'What,' he stuttered, 'what you talking about?'

'Mr Thomas,' I said, 'you could get locked up for this, you know.'

'Me?' he asked, still the anxious father. 'Someone kidnapped my daughter, I'm out of my mind with worry, and now I find out she's safe you're accusing me of some crime? What crime did I commit, Mrs Providence?'

'Sit down, Big-man,' I said calmly. 'Take a seat.'

He found a chair opposite me at the table and sank into it.

'Let me see, Big-man,' I began to count on the fingers of my left hand. '$300 a day plus expenses, let's call it $4000. Small change for a man like you, not true?'

He looked at me as if I was asking for the keys to his palace. 'What?' he cried, 'what are you talking about?'

'Did the story come out in the newspaper?' I said. 'Did you get the publicity you were after, and a fresh set of ex-pats?'

Big-man ran his tongue over dry lips. 'What story? What nonsense you pushing?'

'The nonsense is all yours, Big-man,' I told him, 'the story in Friday's newspaper that someone kidnapped Lynette. Bad news is good news for your business, isn't it?'

'How could the papers print the story? You're the only person who knows Lynette was missing, you and your contacts. And her friends and her boss.'

'Don't forget to add the editor who phoned you at home. You must remember. You wouldn't take the call in front of me. I saw you with the same editor at a reception, you promised him a trip to London.'

Big-man dabbed at his forehead with a handkerchief. 'I didn't speak to any editor,' he mumbled.

'Big-man,' I said, 'this is how the story goes. Lynette and Wray were planning to set up as rivals, so you offered them money. They wouldn't bite, they wanted more. So you got Lynette to "disappear" for a while and hired me to find her instead of going to the police. That way, when the newspapers ran the story, it would stir up publicity, and bring in a whole new set of customers. Big money for you to help clear up with the bank, and Lynette and Wray could have those ex-pats who were prepared to switch.'

Big-man's head flopped. Beads of sweat covered his forehead. The man who once had the newspaper and radio in his pocket couldn't find a single word in the Vincy language.

'My money,' I said, stretching out my hand. '4000 dollars.'

Big-man frowned and gave me a murderous stare.

I suddenly had a better idea. 'Tell you want, Big-man, make it six thousand.'

'Six what?' he growled. 'You mad or what? First it was four, now six, you losing your mind or something?'

'Me? No. But for keeping me here when I should be at home with my husband catching the breeze, think of it as a bargain.'

Big-man got up and came round the table towards me as if he was going to finish what Lynette started. I got up to meet him. In the hot Vincy evening it was glare for glare.

'Six thousand dollars,' I repeated softly. 'I still have contacts in the police force, and some of the returnees are close friends. If the full story comes out, it's once a businessman, twice a shopkeeper for you.'

Without looking, Big-man took out a wad of notes from his right trouser pocket. He tossed it on the table next to me. It could have been six thousand, it could have been the full eight.

I picked the nearest pile of twenties and felt its weight. 'Thanks, Big-man,' I said, 'don't forget your promise. If your business friends get into trouble, you'll know who to mention, not true?'

He grunted, he was done for the night.

Not so his daughter. She pointed a finger at me and waved it, once, twice, before putting it away, like a farmer sheathing his cutlass after warning off a thief.

'Don't think this is over,' Lynette snarled. 'Thomases don't forgive, we never forget.'

I thought of going over and collaring her, but no. I would deal with the threat when it was at my door.

'Good luck, Wray,' I said, slipping the money in my purse. 'Tell your mother I'll be by soon.'

The weekend after he brought me home from the game at Georgetown, 'Vagabond' visited me in Reeves Level.

'Just checking how you are,' he said. 'We had a ranking session in Overland, hot steelpan music, drinks and money for so. Captain Leacock, Farmer Franklin and a fella from Aruba were controlling things, I didn't see you there.'

'Those days are over, Joel,' I explained to him, 'that Cassie was my ugly sister.'

He went silent. Finding me in a quiet mood, he seemed to have lost the touch from the previous Sunday. I fixed him a coffee, we talked about the people at the game and possible venues for the next event. Then we ran out of things to say. When he left I wondered whether he would ever return.

One Friday evening, a fortnight later, he dropped by again.

'Look, Cassie,' he began as I brewed the mint tea I was drinking now.

'Yes?' I grunted, for I was still stuck at the bottom of the crab hole.

'I have something to say to you.'

I sighed wearily, for I just wanted to be left alone to wallow in self-pity. 'Tell away, Joel.'

'I like you, Cassie. I truly like you.'

'Really?'

I couldn't prevent a low groan, for I knew his 'like' meant 'love', and I couldn't see what there was to love in a woman with nothing sliding downhill on her backside.

'Yes.'

'Why do you think that?'

'I don't think it, I know it.'

39

I 'liked' him too, but I was afraid. Afraid to admit my feelings, convinced that he still carried the image of me as the gambler, drinker and wild woman that Sunday morning. Scared that he was confusing pity with love for me, and no woman I know wants that from a man.

'I'm flattered, Joel,' I explained, 'but I can't take you on at the moment.'

'You already have a man?' I had never heard a man so sad.

'No,' I said quickly, so he would know the truth. 'No man. I'm not in a relationship.'

He was even sadder now. 'And you don't want one with me?'

'No,' I said, and raised what I could of a smile to reassure him. 'It's not that.'

'Then what?'

I had resigned from a job I enjoyed, I didn't want to see a soul. Didn't want him to know I was stone broke, didn't want him to feel sorry for me.

'I have some things to work out, Joel. Personal things.'

It was his turn to try a smile.

'No problem,' he said. 'Goodnight Cassie.'

I didn't expect to see him again. I was an impulsive woman, moody, impatient, prone to stupid mistakes. Which man would put up with that?

But one Tuesday not long after, Joel turned up again. It was a month before the Clayton case, and my situation was so grim I was thinking of phoning my father and begging him to come and take me to live with him in Mayreau. I had just dragged myself out of bed, my skin was grimy and sour, my hair a sorry mess.

Some say women act according to mood, then if so, men must act on form.

'I brought you some soup,' Joel said, and this time he seemed on form again.

'Thanks,' I said, 'but I just got up, I need to shower first.'

'Well don't let me stop you,' he repeated in the same confident tone of that first Sunday morning. 'Do what you have to, I'm not moving.'

As I turned on the shower I heard the soft notes of a tenor pan. It was wonderful, the most beautiful music.

I took my time. Shedding the old life wasn't easy. I let the cold water flow gently over my body, soaped myself, then washed the bubbles away. Eventually, wrapped in a brown towel, there I was in the room before him. Joel released the towel, and I stood there mother-naked. No self-consciousness, not a grain of fear. He passed me my clothes and watched me dress. He waited for me to comb my hair back into shape, and I saw the tender look in his eyes.

After the soup it was time to be honest with him. If he could make visit after visit, he deserved the truth.

'Joel,' I said, 'I have something to tell you.'

'What?'

I rubbed my eyes and soothed the frown lines on my forehead. I had no one but my father, and I was about to risk driving away the only other person who had true feelings for me.

'I resigned from the police force some months back,' I said. 'I don't have a job, I can't run my car, my bank book is flat.'

Joel smiled like a man who has played a weak card at dominoes and can't keep it to himself. He gave a little understanding laugh.

'Special Operations. I don't blame you.'

My eyes peeled wide. 'You knew?'

'The force is a close family, Cassie.'

'Yet you kept coming?'

'Yes.'

'Even though I was impulsive and stupid?'

'We make mistakes today, Cassie, but we try to do better tomorrow.'

For the first time in a long while I found a proper smile. It was time to explain to him who I was and let him decide if he was still interested.

My father lived in Mayreau, I told him, he used to be a preacher, but gave it up for fishing. No rhyme, no reason: he got up one day, packed his bible and walked away from his flock. My mother only phoned at Christmas, I had siblings in Trinidad I hoped to see one day. I clowned around in Community College but somehow picked up three good advanced grades in English, IT and Drama; I bored myself stiff in two stores in Kingstown before joining the force. The rest he knew or could guess.

He looked into my eyes, then took my trembling hands and steadied them.

'Let's get married,' he said. 'Then you can tell me what I don't know and can't guess.'

I left Frenches in a hurry. I had to get away from Big-man and his daughter, but most of all I had to get home. Urgently. Through the hot night I thrashed the old Toyota, tasting the saltiness of the breeze and hearing the soft roar of the waves.

Joel was playing his tenor pan when I got in. I showed him the money.

'Six thousand dollars,' I beamed. 'Or eight.'

'Six thousand? Eight thousand? How come?'

I put a finger to his lips. 'Tell you about it tomorrow.'

He put on a CD of him playing that sweet tenor pan. Four o'clock or not, 'Vagabond' had the arms to reassure me.

cassie and the jefferson robbery

My second big case came to me by chance. In many ways it was like the first, where I ended up half-naked in the sea at Indian Bay.

Hustling by the *Music Centre* in Kingstown the Friday morning a fortnight after the Thomas case, I came across this woman with her head in her hands. She was despair self, as my preacher father would put it. Late-forties, 'Portuguese', as we say in SVG, with a light sprinkling of freckles on her plump cheeks, that was the woman in a sleeveless orange midi shift dress looking lost and disconsolate. Behind her glasses her eyes burned like two almonds straight out of hell fire. Her lilac leather handbag sat sadly on the pavement, and the woman was grabbing her head as if a breath of wind, and it might flutter to the nearest cloud.

'No,' she was muttering to herself. 'Lord, no. Tell me is not true.'

I was on the way to pay the monthly bills, but how I could I ignore a woman in distress?

'Miss,' I said. 'You all right?'

She didn't seem to hear me, so I touched her lightly on the left shoulder. 'Everything all right, Miss?'

I saw now that tears were trickling down her face.

'My handbag.' She let go her head and frisked her forearms. 'Where's my handbag?'

I picked up the handbag from the pavement and placed it gently in her hands. She dipped into the bag like she was drawing a raffle ticket, and a white handkerchief wriggled out. Her trembling fingers tried to dab away the tears, I could see it was a struggle to stop herself hollering, 'Murder!'.

'Thank you, Miss,' she said to me. 'Thank you.'

'What's the matter, bad news?'

She gulped, then bit into her lower lip. Too hard, it seemed, for she closed her eyes as if she was eating a sour grapefruit. She needed my help, I could see, I had to step forward.

'Somebody robbed my son,' she stammered. 'Nine thousand dollars. I just took out the money from the bank, and someone hijacked him on the way home.'

'Where?'

'New Penniston.'

'Did he get a good look at them?'

'No. The poor boy didn't see anything. He was in such a state he could barely talk.'

'That is plenty money,' I suggested.

'We have a small gallery in town, most of it is to pay wages, and for materials and travel. Sometimes we barely have enough for tuna and roast breadfruit in a restaurant.'

'I might be able to help.' I was careful not to sound too forward. 'I'm a private investigator.'

She forgot her worries for a while and gave me a quizzical look over the top of her glasses.

'Investigator?'

'Yes.'

She stared now as if I had just told her that the West Indies were sending a rocket to Venus, and I was one of the astronauts for the mission. She gave a weary sigh.

'Makes sense, I suppose. Those good-for-nothing young foreigners they deport from Canada and the USA bring their nasty criminal ways to SVG. I guess it's only natural to have undercover agents.'

'I used to be in the police force,' I explained. 'I set up as a PI a while back.'

She offered her right hand. 'Maria Jefferson. Rudy Jefferson is my husband.'

'You're the *Arts and Crafts* people?'

'Yes.'

I accepted the warm hand. 'Cassie Providence.'

'Mrs Providence, I really hope you can help me,' she said. 'Me and my husband built up our business from the nothing our parents left us, people think we're rich, but tourist numbers are down, we have to watch every silver dollar like everyone else.'

'I'll do my best,' I promised.

Maria Jefferson had the full Caribbean figure, no cutting corners when it came to flesh. With a slightly upturned nose and large but even teeth, she was quite good-looking. If she traded in her square glasses for contacts, Vincy men of all ages might still raise an eyebrow when she swept into view.

'We live in Vermont,' she said. 'Just ask for the Jeffersons, the old house with red galvanize on top of the hill. I'm going straight home. Come by when you finish your business in town.'

'Just a few bills to pay,' I explained. 'How does 12:30 sound?'

'One o'clock would be better. Thank you, Mrs Providence. If we don't recover that money, I don't know what will happen to our dream venture.'

'We'll find it,' I said boldly. 'I'll catch the crooks.'

I walked her to her Jeep, then set off for the centre of Kingstown.

Parmy Denton was a constable during my stint in Bequia.

Five months in Union Island was his next posting, a little bird whispered to him the morning I was packing to go back to the mainland, and smiling from ear to ear. Parmy was young, eager to break up fights, straining to arrest criminals; Bequia was too small and tranquil for his taste.

'Another Grenadine island?' he asked the station sergeant. 'Do I look like I joined the police force to patrol coral beaches and lead home drunk spinsters on Saturday nights?'

Off flew his uniform, on his chest he now sported a shiny travel agent's badge. Parmy stopped me for a chat outside *Voyager* souvenir shop the morning of the robbery. One minute he was asking about Neesha, the next he was trying to sell me a special offer to St Lucia.

'Keep in touch,' he said when I told him to call me at Christmas with a better price. 'This flight-and-hotel package won't come up again!'

But even as we were joking about ten of us swimming at midnight in Port Elizabeth, the robbery was knotting up my head. I was a proper PI now, how could I ignore Mrs Jefferson's call for help? First, though, there was my 'trial' at the market to get through.

My father has his funny ways and, stupid me, I had to choose a man just the same. For a fortnight the kitchen would be like a foreign land, then, one day, Joel would wave me away and take over. A steelpan CD in the background, every pot and pan and knife called into service like the police recruits he trained, for a week he would insist on cooking.

Vegetarian, fish, stew, soup, I would sit in the porch with a novel or magazine, or just soaking up the breeze, and he would serve me his latest 'stew-up' or 'boil-up', the chef with a total of two dishes. Now and again his cooking hit the spot, he would see me nod and the look of delight on my face, and I would spend the night fending him off.

Weeks into our marriage, Joel introduced me to the market woman who supplied the provisions and herbs he used to spice up his efforts among the pots and pans. Mother Hendy from Gomea was his 'sweetheart'. Late-seventies, she was a scrawny leather-skinned woman with a small round mouth and a head of scruffy white plaits. I paid the electricity and water bills that Friday, then picked up two *Nzimbu* banana prints on Bay Street. Always leave the best for last, some people say, or is it the worst? I dragged myself to the market.

'Got you some figs,' Mother Hendy said in her gravelly voice the moment she saw me. 'And some thyme, breadfruit, saffron, bay leaves, linseed, cassava and smoked herring.'

She stored away the cream of everything for me and Joel, so it was always a pleasure to give her a sale – even if the sale often came at a price. We played the same game on every visit.

'You're looking after Joel, nothing for me then?'

She replied with a hearty, woman's laugh. 'You don't need anything, Cassie. You're plump and juicy, nothing in my little herb garden could add to your readiness.'

I grinned weakly. 'It's my husband you love, Mother Hendy, not me.'

'I love him plenty-plenty.' She pretended to be a young belle, patting her white plaits gently as if she was dressing for a show or dance. 'But what he waiting for? When he going to make you a woman?'

I passed over two twenty-dollar notes, adding teeth to my sickly grin so she would spare me. 'Ecclesiastes, Mother Hendy, everything in its season.'

She forced the notes into her purse. 'It's not you, is it? You're not holding him back or locking away some tender womanly secret from your dear husband, are you? Some professional women carry their modesty too far in the bedroom, you sure you're not one of them?'

I picked up my bags to scramble off, the way I always escaped. 'Hurricane coming, Mother Hendy. Listen good, hear the siren warning?'

My car was parked opposite the police station, but even so it was a struggle with my shopping. Heat! Sweat poured down my face and hands. I sat behind the wheel and rolled up the hem of my skirt a little to let the air flow over my thighs. Heat! Murder! But it was no good sitting there roasting. I had work to do, and serious business by the sound of it.

One o'clock was Maria Jefferson's suggestion, but she didn't spend my years in the police force. 'Caribbean Time' might annoy some people – Sergeant De Freitas again – but never turn up at the exact hour. Arrive too early – or better still, late – and you might take home a prettier pearl. So, as I left town I took my time, driving slowly past the beautiful churches, past the Milton Cato Hospital, and up the climb to leeward proper.

In our poems and songs the 'gems' of the Grenadines are magical, but to me they meet their match in leeward St Vincent. Grey sand versus white, I would take leeward's grey sand any day. Volcanic mountains 'sentrying' towns and villages, spectacular isn't word enough for the views all the way to Richmond. Lush green valleys, rippling blue seas, what a fabulous sight before me that afternoon!

There was little traffic on the way, and few people walking. The sun was stinging now, and Vincy people don't need an excuse to take to the shade. From Mrs Jefferson's directions I spotted the house no problem, a mile in from the main leeward road.

I drove past slowly, to log a first impression of the place. From the car I made out tall mango and coconut trees, and the black-green leaves of a plumrose tree. You would pick out this Caribbean landscape in any geography book. I turned by the bridge then drove back, still taking my time, studying the layout. A trickle of a river, a long straight road with a few animals grazing at the edge of the banana field, this seemed too peaceful a place for a robbery.

'Mrs Providence?'

'Yes.'

'You're late.'

'What?'

'You're fifteen minutes late.'

'Who said?'

'*I* said.'

The wiry man who pulled in the iron gate was the same complexion as Maria Jefferson. At least the top half was. His chest was shiny with sweat, his hair a frizzy brown-black tangle that would damage any comb you put to it. A rope was like an understudy for a belt, holding up the black cotton trousers. His yellow wellingtons? Well, why not? As I climbed out the car a smell of beer, cigarette and stale sweat hit me. On the ground to his right, I couldn't help noticing a slim machete sleeping in a yellow coconut.

'And who are you?' I asked.

'Pedro Bowens,' the man said, as if he expected me to recognise the name. 'I'm the gardener, farmer, cook, fixer, driver, I watch over the place. I can turn my hand to anything.'

'Impressive.'

'Thank you, Miss. But nothing for a man who lived here, there and everywhere.'

'Truly?'

'Yes. Trinidad, Puerto Rico, Dominican Republic, Panama, France, I've been to countries most people in SVG can only dream about. The languages I speak will jealous Mrs Keizer, my old primary school teacher.'

I smiled and bowed to the traveller. 'And now?' I said.

'Rich, poor, ugly or handsome, everyone on this earth has to settle down eventually, lady. You travel far and wide, then you have to find yourself a place to call your own.'

'And yours?'

'Not far, just a mile up the road. A little house I built with my own hands and capital.'

He clucked like a hen that had just laid a hot egg. The hen turned into a bony man reaching for the handle of the machete in the coconut. I followed man, machete and coconut, to the bottom of the stairs.

'Ria!' Pedro shouted, and I heard Maria Jefferson answer to give her a minute.

Pedro threw me a grin, and I wondered if he was trying to impress me with his powers. I didn't have to wonder for long. Because, like a teenage vendor in Kingstown on pay day, he placed the coconut in his left hand and, chop-chop-chop-slice, a small round hole appeared in it, like a white mouth in a yellow face without nose or eyes. I *was* impressed. Skill as well as power.

Pedro put the coconut to his mouth. Gulp, gulp, gulp, aaahhhh. The next minute the empty shell was flying above my head onto the pile by the gate. Sweet, cold and refreshing coconut water, what kind of man wouldn't offer a woman a taste on a hot day? I waited for Pedro to close the gate then climbed the stairs.

'Hello again, Cassie,' Maria Jefferson said. 'Good to see you. Guava juice?'

'Thanks.'

She had a tall glass with lots of ice ready, just what I was aching for. She had changed into blue shorts and a lime-green top, and her sandals were airing the neat toes.

'How was the drive?' she asked, leading me to a settee.

'This part of the island is top-ranking.'

'Isn't it just? Sometimes I think they should teach *Beauty* at school. Too many of our people are blind to the splendour around them. Catch the children at primary school, Rudy is always preaching, teach them how to appreciate trees and flowers and insects and mountains. And the sea, of course.'

'My husband would like you.'

'He's an artist too?'

'He's in the police band.'

'Musicians and artists are part of the same family. That's what *Jeffersons* are about: celebrating the artistic talent of the country. Teaching people to open their eyes to our history and geography. Using the raw materials in villages and towns to create art.'

'You and Joel would definitely get on well.'

'Would be good to meet him. But down to business, my son is in his room waiting.'

'Yes, of course,' I said. 'The robbery.'

'Andrew!' Maria called, and a moment later her son stepped out.

Andrew was eighteen, tall, more my black complexion than his mother's. He was handsome, with small, sleepy eyes. I could imagine him wowing girls who go for clever, serious-looking boys.

'Andrew, this is Mrs Providence.'

He smiled shyly, and took the chair to the left of his mother. He went down on it as if the seat had a cushion of eggs. After the damage of the robbery, I imagined he was afraid of adding the chair to his woes.

'Hello Andrew,' I said. 'Sorry to hear about this morning.'

He wore the same lost, sorry look as his mother outside the *Music Centre*. Two grey tear lines were still on his face. I waited until he raised his head then said, 'Tell me what happened.'

Andrew took in a large breath as if he was going to dive deep, then began in a low whisper.

'Mom put the briefcase with the money in the car, I primed the combination lock and set off. The trip was smooth, no worries. No vehicle following me, none blocking the way. Close to home there were these two cows in the road, a bull and heifer. I hit the horn but they wouldn't move. So I got out the car to drive them off.

'When I got back in, I noticed the car was low on gas, so I pulled in at the station to fill up – we always keep some change in the car. I was just reaching for the money to pay for the gas when it hit me that the briefcase was missing. I looked on the floor, under the seats, in the boot, everywhere. Gone. Disappeared.'

Andrew buried his face in his hands and his head dipped. His mother patted his back, and his head rose slowly. I waited for his hands to give back his face then asked, 'So you didn't see anyone at the edge of the fields?'

'No.'

'No one walking along the road?'

'No.'

'Just the animals?'

'Yes. One chewing its cud, the other one mooing and mooing and refusing to get out the road.'

'Do you know whose?'

'No. We keep sheep, pigs and goats, the Toneys have animals, the Bullocks and the Samuels rear too. Others in the district slaughter at weekends, but I don't know where they buy from.'

'Where did the cows go?'

'One stumbled off into the field, I almost had to drive into the gutter to get round the second one.'

'How long were you out of the car?'

'No more than three minutes.'

'Did you get out the car at the gas station?'

'No. The pump attendant came to me for the forty dollars for the gas.'

'And no one came near the car?'

'No.'

'No vendors with a basket of peanuts, golden apples or ice cream?'

'No.'

'Does anyone know your routine?'

'No,' Maria Jefferson answered for her son. 'No one outside the family.'

'Anything else you could tell me?' I asked.

Andrew thought for a while then said, 'No. Only that when I got back to the car, there was a smoky smell like someone was cooking or roasting breadfruit nearby.'

'What about you, Maria?' I said. 'Anything unusual in the past week or month? Any suspicious visitors to the house?'

'No,' she replied. 'Our artists and craftspeople are always dropping by with their work, the people we move with respect what we do. We depend on one another, a steal from one is a setback for us all.'

At that moment another boy came from the kitchen. He was almost as tall as Andrew, and with the same studious look. They could have been brothers, except that one was near to tears, and the other was sipping a cold beer.

'This is my nephew Viv,' Maria explained. 'He's at university in Barbados. His seven o'clock flight got in after eleven last night. You know what LIAT is like.'

I nodded to Viv, finished my guava juice, and, after agreeing fees, Mrs Jefferson showed me out.

On the drive home I stopped at the spot where the robbery took place. The road was narrow, the banana field thick on both sides. Yes, easy cover for the robbers. I decided to drive to the gas station on the leeward-to-town road. It was worth a look there too, a visit might throw up something.

I parked well away from the pumps and sat in the car for a

while. How would I carry out a robbery there? Approach from the rear of the gas station away from the main road? Wait for the traffic to ease, steal up to the car, get an accomplice to distract the driver and snatch the case with the money?

Seven customers were in the shop when I went in, buying ice, plantain chips, biscuits, and lollies. My ears for their chatter, an eye on the youngsters outside, I was the woman hefting the bottles of sorrel jam, guava jelly and tamarind paste. By the roadside I saw three boys and a girl sitting on concrete bricks playing cards to pass the time. Probably *rummy,* a dollar a game, but more likely smaller stakes from the slowness and quiet of their play. Their poses told me all I needed to know, so I bought a bottle of cold mauby and left.

When I got home I fed Joel the ingredients to chew over. Fingers on his right jaw like a lawyer already calculating his fees, he listened patiently. A question here, a clarification there, then my husband gave me his 'theory'.

'The criminals snatched the bag at the gas station. If not there, one of them used the cows to lure the boy from the car, and the other one grabbed the case and ran into the banana field to hide. They must have been watching the house and the Jeffersons for a while, the robbery had real background to it.'

This was my second big case, Joel made it sound easy, but I couldn't figure out where to start. I was Cassie The Impatient then, I got vex with myself quick-quick. Bring me your troubles, leave with the answer, that was how foolish I was. A robbery in broad daylight, on the main road with thick banana fields on both sides for cover; slick job, well planned and carried out; probably two people involved, one the lookout, the other to snatch the case: why couldn't my PI finger point straight to the culprit?

On Friday evenings our little town came alive. Visitors flooded the shops, many in their Sunday best. The moment she got in, Ardene Piddington, a neighbour, would put on her favourite CD, and the noise would blast till she fell asleep, or the children turned it off to do their homework. She was blasting that Friday. Eric Donaldson followed by Fireman Hooper followed by Dolly Parton, we knew every line of the tracks on the CD. Through every song I was making notes on the whiteboard in my office. Names and background of the visitors to the Jefferson home, plus those people I remembered from my police days who favoured this kind of crime. Motives, possible alibis, form, I gave each one a score between 1 and 5.

But the totals came in near the same. Whiteboard, black notebook, not a single link. I couldn't promise a woman and back out, how could I live with that reputation? On Saturday morning, thanks to the music and my impatience, I woke up with a stinker headache than when I went to bed.

Why make such rash promises to Maria Jefferson when the police could put out ten officers to just me and Joel? Was it because it was a woman, or was I trying to live up to what Sergeant De Freitas had told Corea about me? I spent the morning watching the Jefferson house through the raindrops, and snapping Pedro trimming trees, chopping wood, and heaping leaves – just as he had told me. Viv went swimming in Layou when the sun came out, I followed him in the Toyota and took pictures of him and his friends splashing in the sea.

For my troubles I came home that evening with a chill. I felt so weak I threw off my damp clothes and climbed straight into bed. When I got up around nine I saw Joel out on the block with the men playing cards and putting the world to rights. Lucky him. He only had me to worry about, I had him and Maria Jefferson.

I was better on Sunday, but still a bit lightheaded. Joel made me a peppery chicken stew to knock the chill out of me, and it did the trick. I asked him to call the old thief Stephen

Jasper to 'pick his mouth' about the robbery, he was on the phone before I could finish the request. Stephen Jasper was in hospital, he had to shake me from an afternoon nap to tell me, I could cross that name from my book. I was turning over to go back to sleep when Joel said, 'No good locking yourself in the house, Cassie, clues don't seep through the window with the breeze, you have to go out looking for them.'

That got me out of bed: the truth of his rebuke, and the straight face I could see past. There was a domino tournament in Walliabou, Joel was itching for a game, the days when he limed on his own were over. But if you can't go along with your husband now and again, you can't complain if you end up going it alone.

'All right Joel,' I said. 'But back home no later than midnight. This case is truly humbugging me.'

Walliabou was all Stennetts, Woods, Nobles, Olliveres and Goodlucks, old families, many of them Carib descendants. They loved their dominoes, a match could pull spectators from all over the island. Well over a hundred people were drinking and chatting merrily above the music when we got there just after eight, me in three-quarter length black trousers, olive shirt and dark glasses, Joel sporting a purple shirt, stone shorts and sandals. A *Hairoun* for my husband, a malt for me, then we went our separate ways, one to play, the other to work.

It didn't take me long to find someone to 'rounds' with. Leola Lyle, who joined the force a year before me, was on her third beer when I bumped into her grooving by a tent. She was rubbing her stomach gently and sexily with her right hand in a slow reggae dance with an imaginary partner.

'On leave till Wednesday, Cassie,' she got in before I could ask why the slow solo dance, or where her Bajan fiancé. 'Policewomen need release too, you know.'

She blurted out a couple of rude police jokes as she bought me a stout. The official line on the robbery? I didn't have to ask. 'Still in the dark,' Leola volunteered. 'We checked out all the robbers on file, but none of them was near New Penniston at the time. Me personally? I'm sure the thieves did this kind of thing before. If not, the whole country better look out!'

It was after ten by now, hot and sweaty, the kind of night for sitting at home quietly lapping up the cool sea breeze. I was at the bar getting Leola a final beer when I noticed Viv. He was about eight feet away, an older woman in a tight red dress decorating his left arm. To their right a couple, same age mix, part of his party, was one drink away from being arrested for kissing and caressing with intent.

'What happen,' I heard Viv in full flow, 'what happen, a man have to die in here before he get served?'

A quart of cognac and four beers shot up on the counter in front of a grinning barman. Viv drew his wallet from his back pocket and handed him a hundred-dollar note.

'You know what,' he said, tweaking out another hundred, and it was clear that this wasn't his first round, 'double the cognac and triple the beers: nice times just beginning.'

I followed the four to a jeep, well away from the music and dominoes slamming. The light didn't stretch this far, so it was easy to squat in the shadows to watch and listen. But the youngsters hadn't come to the vehicle to count the change from the drinks. I could hear laughing, snorting and loud, fleshy kissing. And even without a breeze, I could smell the women's perfume. Cassie Providence now a village peeping-tom, did I want my name all over the leeward coast? Leave the revellers to their night out, I told myself, Viv had given me a lead. Was he a rich student, or had he come into big money?

Two days later, after checking out Viv's party friends, I dropped in at the *Jeffersons* gallery. It was on Bay Street. The

Jeffersons sold paintings from Vincy artists, and carvings and weavings made from local materials – ping-wing mats, wooden bracelets, goblets from dried coconut shells, necklaces and rings carved from whale bones, conch shells painted in the national colours. They had a small group of craftsmen and women on their books, high standard all of them. Tourists were the main buyers, but Vincies were getting braver and taking a punt.

When I got there at eleven-fifty Mr Jefferson was admiring a seascape. I stood on his right, fingers on my chin, and my head at the artist angle.

'Pretty good,' I purred.

'Not bad for a fifteen-year old,' he answered without looking at me.

'Fifteen?'

'Yes. We had a secondary school competition, 200-dollar first prize. This young man was the runner-up.'

'How much for it?'

'Same two hundred, one-fifty: depends on the buyer.'

'That's a funny way to do business?'

'Get a customer on board and they won't forget you.'

'Still an unusual approach.'

'We survive, Miss. We scrape a small profit each month, but when people in SVG learn to appreciate art, you just watch *Jeffersons* take off.'

Of medium height and build, and with a clean shiny pate, Mr Jefferson was easy to look at when he turned round to face me. The decision to 'go low' with his hair? It could have been the artist in him.

I asked him, 'What do you recommend for a first-time buyer like me?'

'Historical photographs,' he said straight away. 'Verna Soufriere snapped the old sugar mills, collect those. One day they'll be worth serious money, your children will thank you.'

He went to a cabinet at the back of the room, and came back with the photographs, beautifully framed pieces of the history too many Vincies prefer to forget.

'The damage?' I asked, getting out my purse.

'A hundred each.'

'That's a bit pricey.'

'Seventy-five then. Fifty.'

I could see four pictures in our home, and three as presents for friends. 'Deal.'

He wrapped the photos lovingly in several layers of paper, then placed them carefully in a bag.

'You're getting a bargain, you know,' he said. 'My wife says I'm the worst businessman on the island. But in the next year or two, you mark my words, we'll be smashing up abroad.'

It was time to get his take on the robbery.

'I hear you had a little setback,' I said.

'Oh that.' Mr Jefferson gave a small sigh. 'These things happen. Let's pray it doesn't become too regular.'

'Your wife and your son were in the newspapers, they looked pretty distressed.'

'In business you learn to get over trials and move on. No one was hurt, that's the main thing.'

'And Andrew?'

'Andrew is young, Miss, he'll ride it out. He has exams coming up, on Thursday he and Viv will be back at the University Centre revising. Once they get back to their studies they won't even remember the crime.'

'Pedro?'

'Pedro lost his way when he was young. If it wasn't drink it was skirt, he gambled away twice his wages at cards. Show him your shirt and he would bet on how many buttons were missing. Maria plucked him from Satan's grip, he's lucky to have her as a sister.'

'What exactly does he do?'

'He takes care of the animals, looks after the building, keeps the place tidy. Anything to repair, he's the man. I can't believe he's involved: not after all we did for him.'

I thanked him, paid for my pictures and left.

Left for my car, parked on a side street where I could observe the shop. Where, just after one, I watched Mr Jefferson lock up and leave for *Zana's Bar* and a long lunch with two of SVG's upcoming female painters. Pretty women, their hair plaited small and tight, their long flowery dresses dancing in the breeze as if they had music playing inside their bodies.

Hours away from *Jeffersons* didn't seem to bother the co-owner. I made it gone three o'clock before he drifted back. By four he was closing for the day and checking out another bar with a third woman. A basket-weaver this time. A kiss on her cheek to welcome this new one, an arm around her waist to guide her along. PIs spent their days watching people, perhaps artists liked to work with their hands. I left Mr Jefferson to his second afternoon meal and drinks. Vermont wasn't far away, was Pedro bringing home the animals?

Over the next few days I jumped every time my phone went. Suppose it was Maria Jefferson, what would I tell her? That I had pages of notes and closing on five hundred pictures? That I spent day after day studying the snaps of visitors to the house and their gallery in Kingstown and trailing them? What would she say when she heard that I had a picture of every single one of Pedro's animals and theirs? She was paying me good money, how would she take my suspicions about Viv?

I had to be careful what I said about Mr Jefferson too, sometimes a peck isn't a kiss. The women her husband took to lunch, the tight goodbye hugs, was she as generous with their artists? And her brother, the man whose talents could stretch

Anancy's rubber bag, what could I report about his daily trips to the fields with his flock and theirs?

Thursday found me at the University Centre after a visit to the artists Mr Jefferson had spent the afternoon with at the tiny studio they used in Bottom Town. My black PI notebook behind a pile of Chemistry books, I pretended I was a student. I had some of the facts to the case, only they wouldn't let me into their secret.

I was pretending to be a student, Andrew and Viv were the real thing. Heads down, they made notes, sat up to let the ideas sink in, they sipped their bottled water to keep going. Just after one Viv nodded to Andrew that it was time to break.

'Later,' I heard Viv whisper. 'See you down at The *Ridge*.'

The Ridge was an eating place a ten-minute walk away. I trailed Viv, bought a mauby and went over to his table.

'Anyone sitting here?'

'No,' he said without looking up.

I took a seat. 'Thanks.'

He was munching a cake while skimming a textbook so I said, 'Looks like heavy stuff: what you studying?'

'Physics,' he answered proudly, and I knew my face hadn't registered from Friday.

'Where?'

'University of the West Indies: UWI.'

'Hard?'

'Real tough. Especially the quantum mechanics.'

'What year?'

'Second. One more to go.'

'What class degree you aiming for?'

'Two-one. The fees real steep, anything lower would be a waste of money.'

'Money didn't seem to be a problem the other night.'

'What night?'

'At the domino tournament in Walliabou.'

He stopped eating and looked up at me.

'You were there?'

'Yes.'

'And you saw me?'

'Splashing out hundreds, and adding Biology to your Physics. Where did you get that much cash?'

He stared at me, and I could see him trying to place the face.

'You're that investigator woman, not true?'

'Yes.'

'What you spying on me for?'

'I'm a PI, not a spy.'

'Why you interested in me?'

'Somebody robs your aunt of 9 000 dollars, you know the family routine, you're out spending big: how do you explain that?'

'I don't have to explain myself to you.'

'Don't you?'

'No.'

'You don't want to tell me why you didn't go with Andrew to the bank like a good cousin? You're not going to reveal where you got all that pocket change?'

'I got in at midnight on LIAT the Thursday, so I woke up late. I have an exam the week I get back to university so I spent the morning revising. As for the money, my aunt gave me a little extra for placing in the top ten in my last Physics module: satisfied?'

'How much did she give you?'

'Five hundred.'

'That's a good amount.'

'Not really. Double that would be proper money.'

'So it's nice time every night then?'

'Nice time is for *young* people, not for elders like you,

Miss. You had your years, if you missed out on the fun that is your hard luck.'

That stung. I left the mauby right there, best to leave before Viv dished out more licks.

But at last, some flesh to make a proper soup. I knew I was right to track Andrew, Viv, Pedro and Mr Jefferson, log every contact, and add details of their spending. The visitors to the shop and the house were clean, the two women Mr Jefferson entertained spent the nights with their husband and children. The stain of the stolen cash had to be on the hand of one of the four men in Vermont.

The boys studied till twelve each day, then met up with their girlfriends. Andrew's girlfriend was a student too, same age, same clever look. They went to the Botanical Gardens for lunch, for little kisses, holding hands, nothing heavy.

Viv's love worked in *Planning* in Kingstown. She was twenty-five, and he sometimes slept at her place in Queen's Drive. Not one night did they go out while I was watching them: they either had small appetites, or they stocked up on everything they needed in case a hurricane struck the island overnight.

When I was done with the others I went back to Pedro. He tied out his sheep, pigs, cows and goats between seven and eight, you couldn't find happier animals. They didn't fuss during the early morning traffic, his two dogs barked them into line when the noisy vans drove by. After his run with his flock, it was a short trip up the hill to the Jeffersons to collect their animals. To the same shady plot they trekked, to share feed and water.

For the next few hours Pedro worked at the house. Mowing the lawn, picking fruits, planting shoots or fixing the vehicles, my binoculars always gave me the bareback man earning his keep. At twelve he downed spanner, axe, rake or cutlass, and drove to a shop at the old end of New Penniston. He loved a cold beer, he spent eight dollars on the lottery every day, according to the shopkeeper. But beer, lottery tickets and a dwindling flock, was this a man with money to burn?

Petit Bordel, Penniston, Barrouallie, Camden Park, me and Joel propped up the same bars and rum shops the police had their plainclothes detectives in. 'Mix and mingle' was one of the first things they taught us during training, so we listened for names and put up with hours of gossip and political chatter. Every drinker had a theory, each biscuit-muncher could name the suspects. But ask them how, why and when, and they stuffed their mouths with their drinks or biscuits and kept them there.

By now all the island was talking about the robbery. Idle chatter mostly, gibberish, total stupidness, especially on the radio. To hear the nonsense you could only sigh at the blight of people who don't read. Everyone was speculating, I was watching and listening and growing frustrated.

One morning I plucked up the courage to phone Maria Jefferson.

'Things slow,' I told her the truth, 'the robbers keeping low. No signs of anyone larging it, bragging in shop, store or bar, the people who snatched the case playing a patient game.'

She listened, and I felt bad that she was working extra hard at the shop and studio, while I was like a woman brewing coffee with cold water.

'Just do your best, Cassie,' Maria Jefferson said. 'Do what you have to, I know you'll get there.'

Her faith in me put my mind at rest. I was expecting her to remind me what each day cost them, when she didn't, I breathed a sigh of relief. I would catch the culprits, I told myself, you can't promise a woman and leave her dangling. Not when she trusted you.

Viv, Andrew, Pedro, Mr Jefferson, any one of the four could have carried out the robbery. Viv had an older woman to please, if he could fit in his spending and high life with his revision, he could take a snatch in his stride. And Andrew, what was to stop him staging the robbery and taking a slice of the cash? He was a clever student, why not an even better actor?

Mr Jefferson more than doubled the boys. How could he carry on as if losing $9000 was no more than stumping your big toe? Outside of their painting and craftwork, how much did he know about the women he took to lunch? The two I talked to were genuinely upset about the robbery, but did he give away some secret to someone else over a drink?

And Pedro, the traveller, the man of the world, was he happy labouring for the Jeffersons? His stock was down each time I snapped, was someone stealing his animals? Four goats were missing from the Jeffersons' flock too, where did they go?

All these questions kept me up at night, but no suspect put his hand up. The end seemed miles away. A rough day at work was to open up the case.

This was five days later, and I was tired of going through my snaps and notes and trying to identify which animal had said goodbye to the flock. When Joel got in that evening he had a face like thunder.

'Damn recruits,' he grumbled, 'this new batch must be plotting to book me a room in the mental home.'

'Problem?' I asked, for it took a lot to bug him.

'More than that. Some of the trainees don't want to learn to read music.'

'Can they play?'

'Yes,' he said, 'they're naturals, that's why it's so blasted frustrating.'

'Then give them time, Joel. Patience, remember?'

I sat him in the porch and began to massage his shoulders. My fingers dug in, deep, deeper, rougher, till I got him to agree.

'I suppose so,' he sighed.

I eased off the shoulders. 'It's bakes and fried sprats for dinner. Want yours now?'

'Not yet. I need to cool my head first.'

'Fancy a walk?'

'Why not?'

As usual we set off without a compass. We took our time, enjoying the sounds of an evening in SVG when the heat wraps itself around you, and you can hear the sea nodding off. An hour later we found ourselves close to Gomea. Why not drop in on Mother Hendy, Joel suggested.

'Joel, Cassie.' The old woman made the sign of the cross. 'What a blessed surprise!'

She invited us in and offered us a drink, a bitter-sweet brew of aloes and a dozen ingredients she wouldn't spell out for money.

'Cassie, you looking thin,' she said after my second sip. 'My little girl ill?'

'No, Mother Hendy,' I replied, rueing this habit we women have of putting each other under the microscope. 'Your little girl is fine.'

'You sure?'

'Yes. The case I'm working on is a trial. It's taking a lot out of me.'

'Then you need a good broth to keep your strength up,' she said. 'And I have just the things to hand.'

She made up a bag of herbs, and fetched a heavy moonshine yam from the kitchen.

'Old Bowens was round earlier,' she said. 'If I knew you two were going to pass by, I would have got you some fresh beef to go with the yam and herbs.'

I flung off my tiredness like an old blouse. 'Pedro Bowens?'

'Yes.'

'He was here?'

'Yes.'

'What time?'

'About two o'clock.'

'Gomea is a long way from Vermont.'

'He used to live here.'

'When?'

'Seven, eight years ago. That man used to smoke, drink and gamble round the clock. If you dressed a banana tree in a skirt he would buy it flowers. Then one morning his sister and her husband turn up and bundle him into a jeep. He working as a gardener and cook the last I hear.'

'Today was his first time back?' I asked.

'No, he was here a couple of weeks ago. He sold three bulls and a heifer to Givelove Guilding, those animals were healthy and strong, they fetch real money.'

'How much?'

'Couple thousand each.'

'Why is he selling up?' Joel asked.

'He building a basement to his house, they say. Cards, music, liquor, stew pork and fried chicken, in one weekend you could make a killing with a hideaway like that – if you believe what people say.'

I kissed her on the cheek. 'Thank you, Mother Hendy.'

I was in Vermont bright and early the following morning. Pedro would be taking his animals to the fields, I wanted to hear about his spare time job. I parked on a side road and waited for him to go by. The dogs usually came by swaggering and barking, with Pedro and the animals close behind. But farmers went by, nurses, civil servants, schoolchildren, but no Pedro.

I drove up the hill to his house. Just the dogs chasing butterflies, no animals, no jeep. Perhaps Pedro beat me to the clock that morning, I told myself, perhaps he was at the Jeffersons taking their animals out. Either that or a big rock was about to roll down the mountain.

The Toyota answered my right foot, then coasted into the field opposite the Jefferson house. No sign of his jeep there either, no sight of the gardener about to prune trees or mow the lawn, no creaking of falling branches. What the hell was going on? Did I miss something? I was thinking of checking the spots where he usually tied out the animals when my mobile went.

'Cassie, you at home?'

'No. By the Jeffersons.'

'Social visit?'

'Working.'

Parmy Denton was all intrigue. 'Remember that special I was offering to St Lucia?'

'Yes.'

'Well, I just had a taker. Run into town to check my spelling for me.'

I eased the Toyota back onto the road. When the Jefferson house was out of range, I put my foot down.

On the way to Kingstown I phoned Maria to make an appointment. One o'clock, I suggested, why not finish the same time we started?

Recalling Sergeant De Freitas once again, I was at the Jeffersons ten minutes early after my trip to the capital. As I came up the hill, I saw Pedro scurrying to the gate. His hair low, the scruffy beard gone. He had on a yellow shirt, blue jeans and brown shoes, he resembled a man with a new young love to please. Only the cigarette remained from the old Pedro. I parked on the lawn.

'What you doing here?' he asked.

'I have an appointment with Mrs Jefferson.'

'She never tell me.'

'You can't know everything.'

'When you fix it?'

'On her birthday.'

I got out of the car and closed the door. Pedro came up to me, close, very close.

'Mrs Providence,' he reminded me, 'my sister had a robbery, her business losing money, she worried like hell. I hope you're not here to add to her problems. I take it you know what you're doing.'

'I do,' I whispered, as if we were exchanging wedding vows.

'Well, let me give you some advice. Be careful. She fragile right now. If you bring her any more troubles, she might just call me to escort you off the premises.'

He made to get even closer, but I wasn't going to let him have all the fun. I moved to him instead, near enough to smell the rum on his breath. If we were lime-ing, he would have complimented me on my perfume, and promised me another dainty bottle for Christmas.

'I don't need advice,' I told him. 'But thanks anyway.'

He backed away a little, not much.

'This is a close family,' he continued. 'You hurt one, you hurt all.'

'Don't worry,' I answered him with a smile. 'Hurting isn't in my nature.'

I didn't wait for him to show me up. I climbed the stairs and called out, 'Mrs Jefferson?'

As before Maria Jefferson was ready for me. Red and blue smudges on her fingers, she must have been working on a painting. My heart began to race.

'Hello Cassie, how are things?'

'Fine.' I tried to sound calm, but my heart was galloping now. 'How are you?'

'Very busy. Sales are picking up nicely, Vincy people giving us the support we badly needed to soothe our troubles.'

We went to the living room.

'Andrew,' Mrs Jefferson called out, and her son came from the kitchen with a glass of damsel juice.

He was still the shy boy, with a 'Good afternoon' as he passed me the glass. Viv was soon with us too, and my heart started to pound as well as race. It was now or never. I would either crack the case or make a fool of myself.

Maria Jefferson waved me to a seat, the two boys waited till I was down then followed.

'You have some news?' she asked when all four of us were comfortable.

I took a sip of the damsel juice, looked long at each person in turn, then said, 'I think so.'

'Good.' She gave me an encouraging smile. 'Time to clear up this nasty affair.'

The two boys sat forward in their chairs, I eased back in mine

'It was hard to know where to begin,' I made a slow start. 'The robbery was so quick, no witnesses, not much to go on. So what to do? Investigating is about listening, spotting changes. And putting up with getting wet, not to mention headaches. I watched your house and put every visitor on file. The people I didn't know, I snapped and followed home. I tracked Pedro and the animals to the field every morning, I was there when he brought them home in the evening. Always his flock first, then yours. A big robbery like this, and life just carried on as normal!

'Leeward, windward, town, no one could spell out a name. Me and my husband spent hours in the shops and bars just like the police, buying drinks and picking mouths. Gossip, noise, foolishness, a hundred idiots told us a thousand Ali Baba stories.'

Out of the corner of my eye I caught Andrew smiling. Viv? Stone-faced.

'I visited your business in town and talked to your husband. He didn't know who I was, he had no idea I was watching him. In the bars and restaurants, I saw him entertaining your female artists. Did one of them pocket a secret and pass it on to their husband or an old flame?

'One Saturday night I saw Viv at a domino tournament in Walliabou with a group of friends. Drinks flowing, plenty of hugging, squeezing and kissing. Where did a student get so much money to spend? Was he in on the robbery, did someone pay him to keep quiet? He has a woman-friend in town, older, and with a taste for pretty frocks. Was she pressuring him? Did he steal the money to buy her expensive presents and more dresses?'

Viv wasn't smiling now, he looked anxious. I finished the damsel juice and put the empty glass on the table. Mrs Jefferson didn't forget she was a host.

'Another drink?' she asked.

'Can I try the coconut water,' I said. 'Pedro said the trees by the gate are real sweet.'

'They are. I'll get him to pick a bunch.'

Mrs Jefferson got up and made for the stairs. A few seconds later there was a loud crash as if someone had stumbled and fallen over.

'Pedro,' we heard Maria Jefferson shout, 'what the hell you doing behind the door?'

There was a grunt, a groan, and a string of words from a Russian dictionary.

'Get in here,' Mrs Jefferson said. 'What are you now, a macko, an eavesdropper?'

Still in his brights, Pedro shuffled into the room. He saw four people, he gave us four nasty looks.

'Sit down,' his sister ordered, 'come and hear what Mrs Providence has to say. Then pick us a bunch of coconuts.'

Pedro grunted, no one was going to tell him what to do. Not when he had on his new outfit. His back to the living room door, legs crossed, he looked like a man on the way to a fete a week early.

'Then there was Pedro.' I picked up where I left off. 'He's part of the family, you don't keep anything from him. My first afternoon here he even knew I was fifteen minutes late.

'He had the cows well-trained, he coaxed them into the road when he saw the car. When Andrew got out to try to shift the animals, he snatched the case, hid in the banana field, and waited till the car was gone. What did Andrew remember when he got back to the vehicle? A burning smell. The robber was smoking a cigarette, that's where the burning came from.'

I stopped and looked straight at Pedro. He had his arms folded across his chest as if he was going to pick holes in my explanation.

His arms still folded, he gave a small laugh and a shrug. 'So what, lots of people smoke.'

'True,' I replied, 'but not everyone sells off their animals after a crime. Why was that? To explain where you got so much money? Or do you have something else in mind?'

'Who told you about my stock?'

'Nobody,' I said. 'One day you had 21 animals, three days later when I snapped them I counted 19. Last Saturday you only had ten. And four of the Jeffersons' goats were missing. Cows, sheep, pigs and goats don't just vanish into the air.'

'You were watching me? You were following me all the time?'

I shook my head. 'Not all the time, no, I was foolish. If I tracked you at the weekend a fortnight ago, I would have seen you in Gomea, Belmont and Fountain selling beef.'

Pedro burst out laughing. He was still laughing when he bent down to tie his laces. I didn't like it. His new shoes, or his sense of humour. I wasn't wrong. For, before I could continue, he was hurling himself at me. I saw the technicolour bundle coming my way, fast and furious.

I shot up from the chair. When he was close I twisted my body sharply to the left like a matador. I caught him by the back and locked my arms around his stomach. I squeezed him, hard. He grunted and swore, his hands flapped backwards to grab me. I squeezed him harder, he slammed wild fists into my stomach. Too many of his blows were connecting, I trapped his hands, bent him over, and pinned them onto his back. Then, using my right leg under his body, and my right arm, I twisted his body round. After a struggle, I forced him into a chair. His nostrils flared, his eyes went red, but he stayed put.

'Pass me my handbag,' I called to the nearer boy.

Andrew reached to his left, picked up the handbag, and handed it to me. I took out an envelope and passed it to his mother. She looked at the airline ticket then handed back the envelope.

'No wonder you all dolled up.' Maria Jefferson was standing over Pedro now. 'Just look at you. About to fly off to St Lucia with $9000 of our hard-earned money in your pocket. You're nothing but a dirty, stinking thief.'

All eyes turned to Pedro. The man who could speak Spanish and French to back up his Vincy, what would he have to say for himself?

'I'll return the money,' he mumbled, 'I didn't spend it.'

Maria Jefferson shook her head. She was calm, but you couldn't miss the anger and rage within her.

'No, Pedro. Rudy begged me to give you a second chance, me and my husband nearly came to blows over you. And to think that all that time you had it in your nasty mind to rob us!'

'I'll give back the cash,' Pedro repeated. 'And you can have half the sales from the stock.'

'We don't want your money,' Mrs Jefferson said. 'You can go to St Lucia, you ungrateful jackass, you can return to your gambling and drinking: when they let you out of prison.'

I didn't see the punch coming. No warning, nothing. For a second I forgot the months of police training. Be alert! Stay ready! The sickening crunch of a solid fist on the left cheek, Pedro hadn't seen the punch either. He made a sound like an old dog choking on a bone as he tumbled out the chair. Andrew stood over him, silent, mad, his right foot ready to back up the punch with a kick.

'Andrew, no,' Maria Jefferson screamed. 'Don't waste your foot on him! He's not worth it.'

She took her mobile from the table and phoned her husband to explain. After the call Pedro dragged himself from the floor and crawled downstairs still feeling his jaw. When he was gone Maria Jefferson took my hands.

'Thanks Cassie,' she said. 'Thanks for catching the thief, but most of all thanks for stopping that Friday and asking how I was.'

'You would have done the same for me,' I said.

She squeezed my hands. 'Sometimes we so caught up in our own world we forget to look out for others. But I know I wouldn't have hesitated.'

She let go my hands, went to her bedroom and returned with an envelope.

'Don't forget us. Drop by *Jeffersons* whenever you're in town, and tell your friends about the work we're doing. We have to get more people to appreciate our place in history. We have a whole heap of talented people in SVG, we have to encourage them to take their art and drama seriously.'

'I will,' I said. 'Joel loves the pictures of the sugar mills.'

She nodded to Andrew, and her son came forward with a large brown package. It was sketch of me, looking thoughtful and serious. How could I not admire it?

'I hope you like it,' Maria Jefferson said. 'I did it from memory. But when you have time, come back for a couple of sittings and we'll do a proper portrait. And bring Joel along, I would love to meet him.'

cassie and the cutlery set

I came home from work one Monday and found my husband in the porch playing draughts. Not alone, as he sometimes did when the rain was pelting, but with a partner. The man had his back to the road. The oval head without a single grain of hair? On anyone else I would have laughed into my palm at the large granite egg.

They got up to greet me.

'Daddy?'

I always felt like a child calling him this, but what else could I say?

My father had his hands out for me.

'Cassie, look at you,' he said. 'My-my, look at my little girl.'

I saw him glow all over with pride, and I could feel the sting of my warms tears.

My father was fifty-five. Not a handsome man, but a face you would remember and respect when you got to know it. He had forgiving eyes, and a full proud nose that would fit a long-serving headmaster. Round shoulders cut him down an inch to five-feet-seven. He was wearing a thin white shirt, brown trousers that swallowed him up, and overpriced sandals from a roadside vendor in Prospect. The bony ribs I felt under the shirt? Had to be a man crying out for someone to care for him.

As I was changing, my mind began to race. My father wasn't one for surprises, I could set a place at the table for him at Easter and Christmas. Turning up out of the blue in October had to spell more than a word. Was he sick? Did he come to tell us that a Mayreau beauty was going to lead him up the altar? You sometimes hear of some crook robbing a shop on one Caribbean island and hopping onto the next schooner out dressed in a long frock and high heels, and with two grapefruits for breasts: was my preacher father now a fugitive?

I hauled on some purple shorts and an olive T-shirt, something cool for a hot but wet tropical afternoon. When I joined them in the kitchen my father took my hands and looked me over again. He wasn't one for too much hugging, so I had to settle for a squeeze of my fingers.

'Something up?' I asked when he let my hands slide away.

He chuckled. 'What happen, since when a father has to be in peril to visit his beloved daughter?'

'Sorry daddy,' I said, 'just that you're putting the phone company and the post office out of business.'

'You know me and those modern gadgets don't get on. And yes, I got your letters. But when you live alone it's always tomorrow, and the tomorrow after that. Soon two letters turn to three, three run to a pile, and then where do you start?'

A clanking noise saved him making up a third excuse. I turned round and caught Joel lifting the lid of a pot.

'I brought some snapper to make up for my bad manners,' my father explained, and I knew then he was fine. 'Me and Joel knocked up a little broth with my early catch.'

'A *big* broth, you mean.' Joel was already filling the soup bowls. 'Two men, two pots, fifty minutes!'

The six beer bottles on the window ledge he forgot to mention winked down at me: my father was religious, not a saint. And, off duty, my husband didn't take a lot of persuading in anything.

Little or big, the broth was heavenly, a true 'man pot'. Joel's half wasn't hard to spot: eddoes, ochroes, chives, young bananas, tender breadfruit, flavour pepper, his ingredients for what he called 'sexy food'. I caught him eyeing up my naked ankles and feet, it wasn't difficult to tell what was on his mind. Over dinner, my father told us about his fishing, and he listened with pride to my old cases. He was happy for me, but which was it in his voice, sadness or loneliness?

News of his return was soon over the district like a scandal – Pastor Mulraine was back. One Sunday seven years earlier, he had collected his bible and showed his flock his back. The next anyone heard, he was fishing for jacks and robins in Mayreau. But he was among them again, they would take that any day.

A dozen well-wishers turned up at the house that evening, soon it was a struggle to find room for visitors. The Pompeys drove up from Retreat, the Ambrices hired a minivan from Lowmans Leeward. Usually a patient man, Joel had to load the Forbes family from Calder into their car at midnight to allow us to get some sleep.

Friends in the morning, the old and curious during the day, colleagues and those with nothing better to do at night. When the tide of callers looked like it was going to drown us, Joel dragged me into the kitchen. 'How about a "gathering" to get things over and done with, Cassie?' On the Saturday then, we put out an open invitation. I didn't know it would lead to one of my most difficult and painful cases.

My father's friends and colleagues came again, some to be near him, others to take in a little noise and a spot of action on a slow Saturday night in SVG. They didn't turn up empty-handed, bless them, but with fried fish, chicken, and jugs of local drinks. A leeward van dropped off a sack of buns, the guests had all the solids they needed to soak up the oil Joel bought.

Noise, kisses, laughter, hugging, handshakes, just as well Joel didn't put on one of his steelpan CDs. Old Mother Reddock would dance if you clinked two cups, me and Joel together would struggle to break up a Christian party. The loud stories got more boisterous, I gave thanks when the excited faces began to grow tired. 'Come home, Parnel,' I heard one woman whisper to my father as she gently soothed his eyebrows, 'we miss your wonderful "sinful" sermons.'

Many of the visitors had a long journey home, a fair few were elderly. So the goodbyes started at eight, some guests leaving to walk, others hustling to get a van. Only locals were still around two hours later, then, finally, two sisters, Shirley Francis and Estelle Cornwall. The five of us took our drinks to the porch to cool off.

What was high above us would have humbled the stoutest heathen. It was a stunning sight. Trillions of stars, if we had ten lives each, the view would make us pray for yet one more. Somewhere in the vastness, were there people looking out with the same feelings of awe?

A year split the sisters, but they could have passed for twins. Their high cheekbones and small wide-apart eyes gave them a striking beauty. You could spot a hint of Black Carib in their forehead, and, if you got close enough, brown flecks in the eyes.

I wouldn't call either of them tall, more put together with style and care. Solid, Caribbean women, fleshy and proud of it. Their figures spoke loud and clear, you could hear them from a good distance away. Fifty-three-year old Shirley was by my father's side all night matching him rum for beer, Estelle's risqué jokes would have kept the party going if we ran out of food, strongs and juice. Just after ten-thirty a car horn sounded by the gap.

'Time to go, Shirley girl,' Estelle said, 'Gabrielle here.'

'Why you didn't tell me it was so late?' Shirley replied.

'And stop you bodyguarding the pastor?'

'You seeing things, Estelle.'

'Me? Never! My eyes only see what you put in front of them.'

'Pastor Mulraine was telling me about his peaceful life in Mayreau – fishing, sitting and admiring nature, enjoying the quiet and solitude.'

Estelle cackled like a napping hen stoned from a plum tree. 'I never heard shadowing a man called that before!'

'*Conversation*, my sister,' Shirley cackled back, 'we were talking, reminiscing.'

'You of all people should know the price on the head of those words, Shirley!'

'Don't drag up the past. If I go down, I'm taking you with me.'

'If that is a promise, good. If it's a threat, even better!'

The horns blared again before Shirley could play out the scene for their audience of three. A young female voice shrieked in the night, 'You two coming or not?'

'Cut the noise, Gabrielle!' Estelle shouted back. 'Why you so blasted impatient?'

A worried-looking Shirley asked, 'No vans running this late, how am I going to get home?'

Estelle took her by the shoulder. 'Don't be silly,' she said, 'you can sleep in Gabrielle's room. She can drop you home tomorrow.'

My father stood in the warm night gazing at the heavens. He looked thoughtful, lost in wonder, but I caught just a hint of a smile at the playful give-and-take. Did he enjoy the two sisters fussing over him? Did he miss the laughter and gaiety of these two beautiful women when he was out in his boat in Mayreau?

Estelle embraced him and pressed her left cheek against his. Eyes closed, she hummed a romantic tune, a Country and Western ditty from before my time. If they were teenagers, I could imagine her mother yanking her away hard enough to pull her arm out of its socket. Shirley waited for her sister to free herself then took my father's hands.

'It's good to have you back, Parnel,' she said. 'I don't have the words to tell you how much we've missed you.'

I could see Joel raising his eyebrows, and mine did a little dance too.

My father kissed Shirley on the forehead, then we watched the sisters stagger off and tumble into the car. A moment later the vehicle was speeding away.

'Cassie?'

'Yes.'

'This is Shirley.'

'Yes?'

'Could you pass by?'

'Why, is something wrong?'

'The police going to arrest me.'

'What for?'

'Stealing.'

'Stealing what?'

'Sorry, but not over the phone.'

'Where do you live?'

'Choppins. Just ask anybody, they'll show you the house.'

'Give me an hour.'

This was a week later, on the Thursday. I was working on a *WARB* in Rose Bank at the time, tracking a nurse. She was coming home at odd hours of the day, her husband was paying me 'to find out what was going on in his house.' I put away my notebook, camera and binoculars, put my foot down, and got to Choppins just after three.

Shirley's house was small but welcoming. A bedroom, bathroom and kitchen all on one level, and a wide porch. In the spacious yard, breadfruit, golden apple, plum and mango trees. She showed me her pride and joy, a vegetable patch next to her croutons, ferns, dragon's blood, periwinkle, and pink jump-up-and-kiss-me flowers. As with Vincy people and hot sun, as with their pets: snoozing on a chair in the porch was a round, grey cat that had never chased a mouse in any of its nine lives.

A fragrant smell of ferns and hibiscus greeted my nose as soon as I entered the house. Shirley led me to a table with a jug and two glasses of lime juice. My habit was to check out the photographs, and I saw seven: three of a baby girl, and two each of Estelle and Shirley looking more than pretty at a wedding when they were in their forties.

Shirley didn't waste time. 'Thanks Cassie,' she said. 'The policewoman coming back tomorrow.'

'What happened?' I asked.

She sighed. 'Estelle went to the station and complained me for stealing her cutlery set.'

The cutlery set sat to my left on the table like an uninvited guest at a party trying to dodge the host.

'And did you?' I asked.

'Me?' she replied in a heavy, weary voice. 'No, Cassie. People are always wronging me, but I'm not a thief. And I'm too old to start that trade now.'

'But the set belongs to Estelle?'

'Yes. She showed it to me last Saturday. She bought it from some Dominican vendor in Kingstown for four hundred dollars. A waste of money, I can tell you that for free.'

'So how did it get here?'

'I don't know the answer to that. It's a total mystery.'

No woman I know would lug a precious cutlery set any distance, she might even hire a vehicle to get her right to her door.

'How did you get home on Sunday?' I asked.

'Van.'

'I thought Gabrielle was going to give you a lift.'

'She was up whole night studying for her exams, I didn't have the heart to wake her.'

'You could have packed the set in your bag by mistake. If your transport is by the gate revving the engine, it's easy to sling everything in your bag and run to catch it.'

'No.' Shirley was positive. 'It was just me and my handbag coming through my front door on Sunday.'

'And you didn't go back to Estelle's house?'

'No. I was in bed all Sunday and Monday getting back to myself, I felt better on Tuesday so I went to town.'

She was buying my services so I took it she was telling me the truth.

'Who found the set?' I asked.

'Estelle.'

'When?'

'She came by yesterday. We're having a party at the end of the month, we were fixing the menu when Estelle pulled it from behind the sofa.'

'And you didn't notice it before that?'

'Not until she put it under my nose and accuse me of every crime under the sun.'

'Why did she go to the police?'

Shirley got up from the table and shuffled to open a window to let in some cool air. 'Me and my sister have always been up-and-down.'

'Your fault, or hers?'

Shirley came back from the window and dropped into the settee.

'This nonsense is bringing on a headache, Cassie,' she said. 'I need to lie down. I'm not sure my poor head can take it. Can you come back tomorrow?'

'One last question then,' I said, 'who is the baby in the photo?'

She cheered up a little. 'Oh, that's little Louise.'

I didn't say anything to my father or Joel when I got in. Good news spread fast in SVG, bad tidings travel at double the speed, so I assumed they already knew. We had a silent supper that evening, Shirley's plight bugging me, and I guessed it was the same for them.

The sisters seemed so solid at the party, why would Estelle want to slur Shirley? And even if she stole the set, why call in the police? I excused myself, and left Joel and my father playing cards. I was going for a stroll through the town to wind down, I told them, feeling bad that I was deceiving not one, but the two men in my life. I wasn't the only one keeping secrets, but I didn't know that at the time.

Out in the dusk of the early evening I took my time, idling past the churches, and taking in the sea breeze. Noticing a light in Mrs Ada's shop, I bounced in. This was usually the place to catch up on the latest happenings, but that evening there was hardly a soul about. Her thirteen-year old son Maxwell was snoozing on the counter, his maths textbook a hard pillow for his head. A customer shook him to pay for sugar and flour, then his head fell back on the book. Poor boy, I didn't want to trouble him for a candle so I left. I wandered aimlessly for about twenty minutes, trying to cool my head. On the way home, my mind told me to drop by Estelle.

'Caaasssssie.' Estelle spread her arms out wide as if I was

a regular visitor. 'Don't stand out there in the dark, come in, nuh!'

She was wearing long, loose green shorts and a yellow merino. Lipstick too, a light shade of pink. And perfume, subtle, enticing, enough to make me wonder if she was killing time before a late date.

I entered, and found a house similar to her sister's, but with two scented candles burning on the living room table. The kind of candles you would use to take away the smell of smoked herring, or to give yourself a shot of asthma to buy a day off work. Shirley's seven photographs were here as well, and at least double that number of Estelle and Gabrielle.

'It's our little weakness,' Estelle explained when she noticed me staring at the pictures. 'We women can't help our little vanities, can we?'

'Ummmh,' I answered, for what else could I say?

Estelle joined me and stared lovingly at the photos.

'Gabrielle is photogenic, not true? Look at the little baby picture, and the one next to it in her school uniform, and tell me that girl hasn't got an eye for the camera!'

'Gabrielle?' I asked.

'Yes,' she answered, 'why?'

'Nothing,' I said.

She was drinking brandy, she got me a soursop juice from the fridge.

'If Gabrielle had a "politician uncle" in Kingstown like some other girls,' Estelle continued, 'she would be on television reading the news. She has the face and the mind, that young lady. And she's proper tough.'

She wasn't exaggerating. Gabrielle was good-looking, with the best features of her mother and aunt. But what was it about the eyes and the proud nostrils?

'I suppose you heard about Shirley?' Estelle sounded like a

kind neighbour passing on the news that beef was going up to nine dollars a pound. 'Fancy that.'

Sometimes a woman has to pretend, so I was all innocent. 'Heard what?' I asked.

'The police charged her for stealing.'

Pretend once, and you often find you have to pretend twice. The surprise in my voice surprised even me.

'Did they?' I said.

'Yes. They served her a summons this morning.'

'What did she steal?'

'My expensive cutlery set.'

'When did she take it?'

'Saturday or Sunday.'

'A cutlery set is a bit bulky to carry off just like that?'

'No one more resourceful than a thief. People in the habit have their ways and means.'

'Why involve the police? Why not deal with it like sisters?'

Estelle's voice became sandpaper-coarse. 'Because she wouldn't admit she was a thief. I told her that if she confessed I would drop the charge, but not Shirley.'

'So you decided to teach her a lesson?'

'She wanted to pay me for it, but if I let her off now, who knows what she'll put her hands on next time?'

'And you're sure she stole it?'

'Positive.'

'Sometimes if your mind is far away you can slip something into your bag and walk off with it.'

'Not Shirley. Stealing is in her blood.'

'Is it?'

'Yes. Clothes, money, jewellery, you can't hold back my sister. When we were young, pity the man who took a fancy to me. Shirley would fly into a jealous rage, all hell would break loose. I tell you I couldn't buy a pretty dress and hang it up to air out. Next day, the following weekend, we would meet up at some fete, same outfit, or identical hairstyles like a card pair of Queens. No matter what, she had to outshine me! I was in hospital for four days with my appendix, when I came out a little bird caution me my sister was driving around with my mister!'

When accusations fly like that it's only fair to check the other side of the coin.

'What did Shirley say?' I asked, praying there wasn't more to come.

Estelle swirled the brandy in her glass.

'She wasn't driving out with him,' she said in a mocking voice. 'He was giving her a lift to visit me in the hospital! Of all the excuses!'

'You seemed to get on well last Saturday,' I reminded her.

Estelle shrugged. 'Yes, but today is Thursday.'

Whatever the delivery, it seemed as if she had a shot ready.

'Who is Shirley hoping to impress with the cutlery set?' I asked.

Estelle made a tickling laugh like a dull schoolgirl asked to spell the word *cat* by a kind teacher. 'You put the question, Cassie, you should know the answer.'

I stayed for another ten minutes. To finish my drink, and to hear more about their relationship. Bitter quarrels over men went with squabbles over perfume, clothes and earrings, it wasn't easy listening. Or pretty.

'This time, though,' Estelle hissed as I got up to leave, 'on this occasion Shirley crossed the line with her grabbing ways.'

On the way home I wished I was back in the police force with Neesha and Parmy to help me out. With three of us sifting the evidence, someone was bound to throw light on the sisters. But I was on my own, with Joel to back me up when I came to a dead end. I needed help, where was Lacy Luck? Not far away, it seemed, because I got a large dose before I could join my client in the Women's Headache League.

As I was taking another stroll in the dusk the next evening, someone grabbed my left arm and pulled me roughly into a side street.

'Shhhhh!' a female voice hissed as I was catching myself.

The woman had on black everything. A narrow face and glasses below a straw hat were all I could make out.

'You went to see Estelle yesterday, not true?' she whispered.

'Yes,' I whispered back.

'Well, they had a big bust-up on Saturday, all three of them. Late-late the bacchanal finish. Cussing and crying and screaming, total pandemonium! Poor Gabrielle was bawling till six o'clock Sunday morning. Terrible to have a young girl in that state, no matter what her crime.'

The kind 'little bird' was back in her tree before I could thank her or ask her name.

After the party the visitors dropped away. I got back to my work, out came my faithful whiteboard to record the deeds of the two sisters. Their motives and form filled a notebook each. To and from Rose Bank each day I addled my brain trying to work out why Estelle went to the police station to make a case against her sister. What was wrong with a stiff word, or four monthly payments for the silver knives, forks and spoons?

I didn't get far in my figuring, too much about the elder sister was perplexing. A new road march went round and round in my head. 'Why, Estelle, why? Why, Estelle, why?'

Shirley had me scratching my head too. What made her lie that Gabrielle was up late studying for exams? And the bust-up, what was that over? Did Gabrielle have a young man in the background? Was the impatient young woman pregnant? Was that the cause of the argument?

Any mention of the sisters had Joel and my father shaking their heads. A spiteful Estelle didn't seem to fit the popular woman liked by everyone. How could two people be so happy together one starry night and at war days later? I told Joel I was acting for Shirley, but I didn't say anything to my father. A gut feeling warned me that he was mixed up in their affairs.

The sisters sent him figs, mangoes, plantains or soursops, Gabrielle sometimes delivered cassava bread and coconuts after work: from her aunt or her mother with compliments. Friends, good friends, just how close were they to my father? He didn't mind them interrupting his work, when they phoned he took the call in his bedroom and pulled in the squeaky door. If he signed off with kisses I didn't hear, I was too embarrassed to listen.

One early morning, on the way to the shop for fresh bread, I couldn't let the question continue to heat up my brain, so I plucked up the courage to ask him. I had to nice up the question of course, some things you just can't put to your parents.

'Daddy,' I stammered, 'when mother walked out, did Estelle and Shirley look after you?'

He answered with an ugly grunt; I wasn't the only one feeling ill-at-ease. But put one question, why not put two?

'Were you one of the men in their lives?'

Another grunt. But when my father realised I was like a batsman thinking about scampering a third run, he held up his hand to stop me.

'Was a long time ago, Cassie,' he said. 'I was friendly with both women and, come what may, I will always have a place in my heart for them. It's not easy watching them bicker like this, but we mustn't cast stones. We mustn't be too hasty to judge – unless we are prepared to face judgement ourselves.'

When it came to the sisters he was evasive, then, but I didn't hold that against him. He was a preacher, but why should that stop him being a man of flesh and earthly needs? As a girl I saw the hurt and bewilderment in his eyes when my mother packed her suitcase for Trinidad and ordered a taxi; *she* was married and settled now, why should he let his life peter out to old age?

Was he lonely? I didn't think so, he didn't look it. Now and again I caught him sitting at the back of the house staring at the Caribbean Sea, but what was wrong with that? After all, I did the same when I didn't feel myself. Sea-gazer or secretive, it was good having him around. After store-jobs in Kingstown that ate up my monthly travel costs, he was the person who persuaded me to join the police. There was a meal waiting when me and Joel got in from work now, his *History of the Spiritual Baptists in SVG* by his pillow next to his Bible, if he missed Mayreau he didn't show it.

Every Vincy I know has a favourite spot on the mainland or the Grenadines. A place full of loving childhood memories, or somewhere to sit and enjoy the serenity. Joel will trek to the volcano seven days a week if he could find good company, Fort Charlotte is my inspiration. For my father Owia is the place. So no surprise then that when he wanted to teach me to swim, we ended up at Salt Pond.

I wasn't a good swimmer, and my father was going to see to that. A fisherman now, his daughter wasn't going to dip her big toe in the sea, get out the towel and dry herself like a town-girl. I had to learn properly, 'dry land' was for those Vincies who didn't move from their precious verandas. That Saturday, on my day off, we drove to Owia Salt Pond, just the two of us. Joel's band was rehearsing, and Sergeant Stoute and the other musicians never finished a session without a toast to the police force.

I liked Owia. People shared what they had, the scenery at the foot of the volcano is magnificent. We paddled a bit in the pond, admiring the volcanic rocks that sealed in the pond, and the pretty fish the goggles magnified. My father was teaching me to float on my back when I noticed a small black weal above his left knee. This simple 'spot' was to open up the case for me.

But first there was Shirley to suss out. Estelle was local, I saw her every day. If I didn't see her, I heard her voice round some corner, arguing, laughing, full of the afternoon or evening. Miles away in her adopted village, something about Shirley's life didn't square – it was too level. My employer or not, I decided to dig into her affairs, her secrets were holding me back. So when the security guard pulled back the door the following Monday, mine was the first step into the National Bank.

I slipped Shirley's name under the counter to one of my contacts, Gwen W. She tapped on the keyboard, looked up in amazement at the computer, and a minute later she was leading me to a back room all hush-hush. In confidence, of course, no money passed: when we met up off duty she would eat till she could eat no more.

In the office Gwen W turned the screen to show me. 'Two hundred dollars a month for eighteen years, Cassie.' She kept her voice low. 'Just seven withdrawals. That is a whole heap of money! Some woman that!'

I thanked Gwen for her help, but I came out of the bank even more confused than when I went in. With over thirty thousand dollars and loose change in her green book, why would Shirley steal a cutlery set when she could afford to buy a restaurant?

After the bank, it was a trip to Choppins to see what else I might stumble upon.

Shirley's house was locked. Junep Mackintosh, her sixty-year old neighbour, was riding the breeze in her porch when I stopped to say Good Afternoon. That is the Vincy way, especially when you're working up to a pry. After taking me through two albums of her children and grandchildren in Tortola, she agreed to tell me about my client.

'Shirley live peaceful.' Junep seemed the protective type. 'Since she move here twenty years ago, not a bad word cross her lips.'

'Visitors?'

Junep gave a hearty laugh. 'No "sweet-man" pulling up by the house in fancy car, if that's what you mean. Unless he sneaking in after midnight and leaving before sunrise!'

'Does she mix?'

'You have to in Choppins, unless you want to spring enemies left, right and centre.'

'Close friends?'

'Just me and Nyoka Neetly. We go to the same church – three women, three quiet lives.'

Shirley helped out at the primary school on Mondays, my tracking also found out, tending her flowers and vegetables took up the other four days. Carrots, cucumbers, onions, thyme, and garlic fetched a fair price at the market in Kingstown, but enough to fill her account?

I arranged to meet her at the Botanical Gardens on the Tuesday, with a photocopy of her bank book in my handbag as back-up.

'My case is coming up soon,' she reminded me.

'How are you going to plead?' I asked.

She was paying me for the case, even so I was surprised at the bad eye she gave me, and the rough answer. 'Not guilty, of course!'

'And the set?'

'I will ask them what use I have for fancy cutlery. It's not as if I have someone to entertain.'

'Don't you?'

If there's such a thing as a sad laugh Shirley gave one. 'You mean your father? Those days are gone, Cassie. Long gone.'

'You're both single,' I said.

'I had a bad life,' she said, 'I dragged down those I loved, I turned away those who cared for me.'

I had to ask it. 'Like who?'

Shirley looked like a woman prepared to plead Guilty to a charge of making mistakes, if not stealing.

'I was a good-looking young woman, Cassie,' she said with a rueful sigh when she found her voice. 'I could make men hop barefoot from country to Kingstown on hot tar. And back again, if I told them to. I had the power, the gift. Rich, on-the-rise, big-bone, slim-body, none of the flatterers could measure up to me – I told them that to their face. The man for Shirley had to build of material from all of them. Eighteen, twenty-one, thirty, I waved each suitor away, even those who probably truly loved me. I wasted my life waiting for a melody no band in St Vincent and the Grenadines could play.

'Stupid Shirley. Most of the men were playing me too. They locked on to my figure and my face, it was their play against my game. Sometimes a woman needs a man to shake her up and tell her to commit to him. To put him first, or on the same level as herself. None of them took the time to do that. I let each one stay a while, then kicked him out with his bundle. And see where I am now? Man-less. And yes, lonely.'

'Estelle?' I asked.

'Every mistake I made Estelle had to double.' Shirley didn't sound bitter. 'We waved away the serious men with the chaff, and now we swim in the same shallow pool.'

'Lots of men about.'

Shirley took my hand. 'Not all men are men, Cassie. You have a good husband in Joel, you're lucky you won't have to learn that bitter lesson.'

I felt like a mullet flapping on a riverbank. First Estelle, now Shirley, same song about them fighting. Two women honest about their jealousies, why did I feel they were only feeding me half the story? All the while my father was in his bedroom reading, quiet, and meditating. It wasn't Christmas, Easter was years away, no way was his sudden appearance an accident. As I sipped a cold lime juice later that afternoon, I cursed myself for taking on a case so close to home.

Four days later my Toyota broke down. The engine suddenly cut out and, every time I turned the key, it made a sound like a sheep staked out in the midday sun. If at that moment it started to pelt with rain, I would have stood there and accepted the soaking. Just my luck, that was how I was feeling. I was fetching my bag from the vehicle when a car pulled up and a familiar voice bawled out as if in song, 'Cassie, what happen?'

Before I could catch myself, Estelle was dragging me into Gabrielle's Datsun. 'Gabrielle,' she was saying, 'Cassie coming with us, you okay with that, not true?'

I thought I heard a low mumble from Gabrielle, but Estelle probably had better hearing. As the Datsun pulled away, I prayed that my car breaking down wasn't a bad omen.

Young Gabrielle was a good driver. When she blocked the vans aiming to overtake three cars in a row, I almost clapped her. In the back seat Estelle and Shirley were all dolled up, thick hair sweetening the breeze, perfume from north to south. Were two lucky men oiling their locks and getting ready to take them for some swimming and dining in the Grenadines? If a little bird chirped that the two people laughing and joking behind us were in the middle of a court case, you would get out your slingshot, aim hard, and spread feathers across the sky.

The sisters had to be mocking me. As the car eased along the coastal roads, that idea came to me and wouldn't go away.

They were having a bit of sport with Cassie. The 'cutlery steal' and the police case? Just a 'cook-up' between them to get them centre stage again for a while.

With her bank balance Shirley could easily afford the $250 a day fee to find out how the set ended up in her house. But wasn't the strain on her face real? Or was I seeing what she wanted me to see? After twenty minutes the car pulled up in Stubbs, and the women got out.

'Drive carefully,' Shirley said to us, gently tapping the side of the car twice.

Estelle gave us a salute. 'Have a safe trip you two. Watch out for the traffic.'

Gabrielle nodded, and her passenger did the same. She let them cross the road, then rolled the car gently down the hill.

'Where are those two going this hour?' I asked, after half a mile.

'To see Verro Moses,' Gabrielle replied.

'A bit early to visit someone.'

'Mrs Moses is a busy woman. If you don't get your order in on time you might lose out.'

'Order for what?'

'Cakes. She's the best this side of the island.'

'What's the occasion?'

'My twenty-first.'

'Oh,' I said. 'Congratulations.'

'Thanks.'

'How are you going to celebrate it?'

Gabrielle eased off the gas. 'Didn't you get your invitation?' she asked.

'No.'

'We told Pastor Mulraine a while back. I was there when mother asked him to invite you and your husband.'

'He didn't say anything.'

'Never mind. I was twenty-one in April, but we're having a do next Sunday. Hope you can make it.'

'Thanks,' I said. 'Save spaces for two.'

We were slowing with the Kingstown traffic now. I asked, 'What do you do, Gabrielle?'

Gabrielle took her time before replying. 'I was studying to be an accountant.'

'Good career,' I said, the way you do when you're making conversation but not truly listening.

'The exams are real tough.'

'But you get a hefty salary when you qualify.'

I didn't catch the frustration in her voice, but I couldn't miss the sigh now.

'I dropped it last week,' she said. 'The tests were making my hair fall out.'

'Sorry to hear that.'

'All those blasted percentages, it was like being back at college.'

'What are you going to do?'

'Switch to Law. Put in for a scholarship.'

'And if you don't get one?'

'I'll just have to find some way to pay for the course myself.'

'Brave decision.'

'Perhaps. But if Law doesn't work out, something else will turn up. Right now, all I want is for this party to go well. Too much strife in our family.'

'What strife?'

'The court case. Your father told you, I suppose?'

'I heard the rumour,' I said.

'It's not rumour, it's fact. Could you believe those two?'

'What did they do?'

'It's a long story, Cassie, and they only feed me bits. Do you ever get the feeling a big explosion coming? Well, take it from me, what they're holding back will be like the hurricane last year!'

Gabrielle was in a talking mood, why not push a little harder?

I asked, 'The night of the party, what was the argument about?'

She gave a nervous laugh then asked, 'You got that news as well, did you?'

'Yes.'

'I'm still trying to fit it into my head.'

'It was that bad?'

'Worse. The lies those two have been telling me all these years. The pretence!'

I didn't realise the car had left the main road until I made out that we were in Choppins, and Gabrielle had stopped outside Shirley's house.

'Won't be long,' she said.

A couple of minutes later she was back with a pile of textbooks. She hurled the books onto the back seat.

'Goodbye profit margins! Hope we don't meet again, Accountancy!'

'You're a brave young woman,' I repeated as we got going again.

'Brave or foolish, sometimes you have to run with your mind, not true?'

With my history, how could I disagree?

'You take a chance and hope for the best,' I said.

'So I'm going to follow your example.'

'Good luck,' I wished her sincerely.

'Thanks,' she said. Then she asked, all excited, 'Where are you working today? Being a private investigator sounds glamorous for so.'

I smiled, wondering if she had any idea what a PI did. 'In Rose Bank.'

'I would love to be in your shoes,' she said.

I hoped my reply wouldn't disappoint her.

'If you enjoy long hours sitting in a hot car with your binoculars on some woman's front door, no problem. If you don't mind trailing some madman across the country, hoping he doesn't spot your vehicle and come at you with a big stick, you can give it a go.'

Just as well she was driving. She was breathless with excitement now.

'I can handle that,' she purred. 'And when I'm a lawyer, I might help you out with a poisoning or a forensic!'

I smiled to myself. Why should youth see obstacles just because adults do?

'Thanks. Leave me your number,' I said. 'But my car is sick so I'm going to make the most of my day off.'

'I was thinking of getting my party dress later,' Gabrielle said, 'how about helping me find one?'

The Rose Bank case was coming to a close, I could spare a couple of hours. But first I had to check if Gabrielle had any more surprises up her sleeve.

'Who's on the guest list for your birthday celebration?' I asked.

'Just a couple of friends from college,' she answered.

'And your boyfriend?'

'What boyfriend?'

'Man-friend, then?'

'Which man?'

'Never mind.'

We met up at twelve by the wharf, at the boutique of one of SVG's best designers, Brenda Hadaway. Her clothes were pricey, definitely for special occasions. Gabrielle loved bright colours, and cuts that exposed skin. With her fifth try-on, a flowery Ghanaian print dress, if she had a wealthy father she could twist round her fingers, I could see her splashing out real dollars.

'What you think?' she asked, treating me to twirl after twirl after twirl.

'It's beautiful,' I said truthfully, for she had her mother's enticing figure.

'Three hundred and fifteen dollars.'

For a Hadaway it was a bargain. 'Not bad,' I said.

'If I had the legs I would go in for the same style, but just above the knees instead of below.'

Up rolled the hem from the knees, like a girl preparing to cross a river.

'Something like this length,' she said.

I took a step back to consider the fit of the dress. And then a second step. And a third, to make sure I wasn't seeing things. For on her left thigh sat a small weal, like a moustache in the wrong place.

'What happened to your leg,' I asked, 'you bruised it?'

'It's a birthmark,' she said, letting the hem of the dress fall. 'It used to bug me so much, I used to hate undressing in front of other girls. But it doesn't bother me so much now.'

'I see,' I said, for at least one thing made sense.

Gabrielle tried on a green sari, then a light-pink trouser suit. A $100 deposit on the Ghanaian outfit settled things.

She was meeting a friend after work so, after a trip to the market, and an hour in the police bar playing cards and catching up on the latest news, I phoned Joel to pick me up. As I was waiting for him by Thomas Saunders Secondary, my father phoned.

'Cassie,' he said, 'you still in town?'

'Yes.'

'Got any cash on you?'

'Yes.'

'We're going to Louise's birthday party on Sunday, could you buy her a present for me please?'

'Who?'

'Gabrielle. Get her something nice. Some earrings, a bangle, a ring, a chain, something like that: you know more about these things than me.'

My car breaking down wasn't a bad omen after all.

Gabrielle's big day was a bright Caribbean Sunday, lazy and slow. After a week pouring sunshine over the islands, who would envy old *Mrs Time* a rest? Mother and aunt had booked a restaurant near Mount Wynne for eight, including two of Gabrielle's friends. Strictly local food, they said proudly, no Irish potato, macaroni pie, pizza or chicken wings, not a grain of rice in sight.

Estelle and Shirley were dressed as Carib warriors, and sported colourful headties. Small silver plastic swords tucked down the waist of their skirts, they looked magnificent. If this was a dance, after what Shirley told me, I could picture two lines of men hopping on one leg just to get a chance to say hello.

Joel came in a brown jersey and navy-blue trousers, I had on a simple white cotton dress. I had combed out my hair until it was soft and round. Not quite an afro, but good enough for a woman who didn't straighten her hair. In blue jersey and brown trousers, my father reversed my husband. But what a star, what a beauty! Cherry-black lipstick, hoop earrings, her hair in fine plaits piled into a high bun, step forward Gabrielle!

Like Anancy's children we climbed into the food. When our stomachs could stretch no more, we found room for sweet-potato pudding. After lunch, a swim, and a stroll along the beach, it was time for cooler clothes. I changed into an aubergine merino, black shorts and sandals. The first step down from the changing room, and there was Joel eyeing up my legs and naked feet again. Three weeks with my father in the next room were beginning to take their toll on him. My own skin tingled like hell, I knew the torment he was going through.

'Stop looking at me like that.' I planted an ugly wet kiss on his lips. 'Or I'll go and complain to your mother.'

Joel tried to grab me by the waist, but I was already dashing along the beach howling at the top of my voice like a mad woman.

Then it was time for the gifts and speeches. We toasted Gabrielle, and kept on cheering when the restaurant owner supplied complimentary champagne. The day was going so well I expected Estelle to turn to Shirley and take her hands. 'Sorry, sister,' I could almost hear her say, 'tomorrow we'll go the station and cancel the stupid charge.'

For it seemed to me the kind of day for making up. I had closed the case at Rose Bank, and I wanted this one finished too. 'She suffering with morning sickness,' a nursing colleague whispered to me for five crisp twenties. 'What kind of man doesn't know his wife is pregnant?'

The Rose Bank cheque safe at home, it made sense to clear up this case too. And quickly. Suffering could become contagious, the sooner we put things right the better.

Gabrielle's friends went after the speeches, leaving six of us in the restaurant waiting for the weather to cool down before setting off home. Shirley had this sad, distant look now, I noticed. Had to be the case. Or was it the thought of Gabrielle becoming a young woman? As I was wondering this, she fetched an envelope from her purse and passed it to Gabrielle.

'From me and Estelle,' she tried to sound merry. 'To make up for the last few months.'

This extra gift on top of a bagful of presents surprised the birthday girl. Gabrielle was all over the envelope, ripping and tearing it. I hoped she would be gentler with her law gown.

'A cheque!' she shrieked. 'Three thousand dollars?'

'To help with your new course.' Shirley brushed Gabrielle's cheek tenderly with her fingers. 'From both of us.'

Gabrielle was up doing a little dance, feet only, no waist, nothing to make a relative blush. When the reel was over she hugged her aunt, then her mother. It couldn't last. As she sat down she spoiled the mood by bursting into tears.

'Thanks mom, thanks aunty. When I gave in the job I was afraid you would be vex with me. I know I can be a good lawyer, I won't let you down.'

The sisters nodded that they were behind her. But their backing wasn't enough. For Gabrielle's face suddenly changed from happy to serious.

'My course starts next month,' she said, 'I want to clear up this nonsense before I leave.'

I saw the sisters' faces tighten, and, to my left, I heard my father cough nervously.

'Not today,' Estelle begged. 'Don't spoil a wonderful occasion.'

But now that she was properly a young woman, Gabrielle was a woman. She shook her head slowly. Five times, six, seven.

'No. I want the *whole* truth. And now, not on my wedding day.'

The sisters fiddled with their swords, I wondered who or what they were about to slay.

'Another time, Gabrielle,' I said when I could hear the waves rolling up to the shore a third time. 'How about Wednesday?'

But Gabrielle was already the lawyer. 'Why? Only family and close friends are here, why not sort it out now?'

Like a man trying to hold off a hurricane with his bare hands, my father joined in. 'There's a time and place for everything. Are you sure this is it?'

Gabrielle wasn't backing down. 'Yes, Pastor Mulraine. My twenty-first is the right time, this beach restaurant is the perfect place.'

Shirley could sense the storm coming too. 'Louise,' she said, 'Parnel is right. Let's wait and fix things in private.'

Gabrielle came and stood in front of me as if I was a juror to sway. She said, 'Did you hear that, Cassie? Gabrielle, Louise: which one am I? You know about these things, why not explain what's going on?'

'You're sure you want to hear it?' I put it to her, wondering if she appreciated the true thickness of the rope.

'Yes,' Gabrielle insisted. 'Good news, bad news, you have to ride with them, don't you?'

She sat down again, and I turned to face mother, aunt and daughter.

'Well,' I began, 'the trouble started after the party. When Shirley and Estelle got home they had an almighty argument.'

I took an early pause. To balance my thoughts, and to let the silence tell them there was no turning back now.

'Shirley was tight,' Estelle broke the silence. 'She was falling over and making a fool of herself.'

'I had too much at the party,' Shirley explained, 'I'm not really a drinker, the occasion got to me.'

'And Gabrielle went mad.' I followed Shirley. 'And lost her temper.'

Shirley looked like she would break under the memory. 'Gabrielle said I was a disgrace.'

'And then,' I continued, 'one of you told her the secret you've been hiding all these years.'

I heard my father cough again, and Joel's elbow jabbed into me as he sat up to listen.

'It just slipped out,' Estelle said in a voice choking with emotion. 'We didn't want her to find out like that.'

'That Shirley is her mother, and not her aunt,' I said.

'Yes. I told her not to speak to her mother that way.'

'And that's why she cried all night,' I said.

'We let the secret fester, waiting for the right moment. But when is ever the right time?'

Gabrielle buried her head in her hands but she didn't cry. I could hear my father breathing heavily, but what has to be done is best done properly.

'At first I thought it was Estelle who planted the set,' I explained, 'but it was Gabrielle. When she found out the truth, she decided to take revenge on her mother and her aunt. They were always arguing, why not play on that? She has a key to the house, she used to study there, what better way to get back at them?'

Gabrielle was crying now. 'Sorry Mommy,' she said. 'I didn't know aunty Estelle would go to the police. I thought she might get vex, the two of you might keep malice for a day or so, and then patch up.'

As the sea breeze poured over us, the sisters moved closer to Gabrielle. Shirley reached out and took Estelle's hands. Estelle closed her eyes tight like a mother waving goodbye to a daughter leaving to set up home with the village womaniser. Why had *she* brought up Gabrielle, couldn't she have children? What was the arrangement between them?

I didn't have the answers. But if lawyer Gabrielle put a further question, I was ready. And she did, it didn't take her long. She wiped her eyes with a handkerchief then said, 'And now my father: who is it, mommy?'

'Please Louise,' Shirley begged, 'enough revelations for one day.'

But spare the mother, ruin the child.

'No.' Gabrielle was easing up on no one. 'Don't just give us the opening chapter, tell us the whole story. Why did my dad leave the country? How come he doesn't write or phone? We have a dozen pictures in the house, but not a single one of the man who brought me into the world. Don't you find that strange?'

Shirley trembled like a woman suddenly whipped by a cold night breeze. 'Give me time, Louise,' she pleaded, 'I need to think.'

'No mommy, break the news. I will just have to accept it, won't I?'

Shirley's mouth opened, but nothing came out. It was time to rescue my client.

'Gabrielle,' I said, 'could you stand up?'

Gabrielle turned to me, half-interested, half-confused.

'Why?' she asked.

I waved her up gently with two fingers. A puzzled look on her face, Gabrielle rose slowly. I stood up as well. Her afternoon change was a long pleated green skirt and a light-blue blouse.

'Your skirt,' I said. 'Show us your left leg.'

'What?' Gabrielle screeched, as if I was a schoolboy too eager to get to Advanced Biology.

'Hoist your skirt,' I said to her. 'No need to be shy.'

She gave me a heavy frown that said she would never trust me again if I embarrassed her. Then she slowly drew the skirt up a couple of inches.

'Take a look at *my* leg,' I said.

Gabrielle glanced at my head, my neck, then my chest. She might have been too embarrassed, perhaps she had forgotten where to find my legs. When she remembered, the hem of her dress dropped abruptly, and her hand raced to her mouth.

'Oh my God!' she wheezed. 'Oh no!'

'Your father has been sending you two hundred dollars a month for years,' I explained, 'but your mother was too scared to tell you. Your aunt calls you Gabrielle, who else calls you Louise?'

My job was over so I sat down. The others had to do what they saw fit. My father got up from his chair as Gabrielle took her seat.

'Louise, I'm sorry,' he said. 'One day me, your mother and your aunt will explain. And I hope you will be able to find it in your heart to forgive us.'

He made to take her hand, but hesitated. Then, finding the courage, he reached out a second time. Gabrielle's hands were resting in her lap, she allowed him to take them. Then she rose slowly and looked him directly in the eye.

'Are you truly my father?'

'Yes Louise, I am.'

She threw her arms around his neck and began to sob. For a good minute she remained like this, clinging to him like a child scared of the dark. My father closed his eyes tight as if he was saying a silent prayer. Was it relief? Joy?

When he opened his eyes, he kissed her lightly on the forehead. Then they sat, Gabrielle next to me, and my father to her left. I put out my hands and took hers. She gazed at me shyly, like a little girl lost on an errand to buy matches, but suddenly recognising a familiar house or tree. My sister!

'You see,' I said, 'daddy didn't just come to visit me and Joel. He came for your birthday party.'

Together now, on the opposite side of the table, Estelle turned to her sister.

'Forgive me, Shirley,' she begged. 'Say you forgive me.'

Shirley nodded, and you could see that she was sincere. 'It's time to forget the nonsense,' she said softly. 'Time to set fire to those pages of our lives.'

We didn't have time to reflect. A sudden blast of a trombone saw to that. I looked to our right and gasped. The next thing I saw was Joel covering his eyes with his hands. 'Oh no!' I heard him sigh softly. I hadn't seen Sergeant Stoute for months, what was he doing here in uniform with his trombone?

Stoute was a hard-drinking, strapping bachelor, six-feet-three and 210 pounds, with thick black hair and a military bearing. He nodded Good Afternoon, then placed the trombone gently on the nearest table.

'Which one of you ladies is Estelle?' he came right to the point.

No answer.

'Could Estelle please identify herself.'

Estelle raised her right hand slowly, like a schoolgirl afraid to correct a teacher having trouble spelling *Guyana*. 'I'm Estelle.'

Sergeant Stoute nodded gratefully. 'Thank you. But I'm afraid I've come to make an arrest.'

'But?' Estelle bleated. 'But?'

Stoute looked down at her through his shades. 'Lady,' he said, 'do you know what we say in the police force?'

Estelle didn't answer.

'We say arrest those people who don't appreciate how busy we are. Arrest them! Jail them! Let them stare at the sea all day until they go mad!'

The restaurant owner brought Stoute a beer just then, and, knowing his habits, Joel nudged me and whispered that he had probably made a short stop at every bar on the way to Mount Wynne.

'I should be at home writing up my reports on a blessed Sunday, but where am I instead? Settling domestic disputes!'

'But,' Estelle said, her third in a row.

When he was charged, Sergeant Stoute was like a warrior.

'Up!' he ordered her. 'Let me show you what I do to those who make me miss my Sunday meal!'

Estelle got up, and now she found the courage to look directly at the officer. She didn't know his reputation, but it didn't take her long to realise what the dark glasses masked.

'What's your name, Inspector?' she asked politely, as if he had helped her cross the road in heavy traffic, and she was about to recommend him for promotion.

'Stoute.'

'Number?'

'4567898763.

'*Police* number.'

Even as she said this, Estelle was filling a plate with breadfruit, stew pork, bananas and lentil peas. She offered him the plate.

'Here, Inspector. Won't you take your Sunday meal with us instead?'

Stoute eased himself onto the bench next to her.

'Thank you, Lady,' he said. 'But let this be a warning to you: the police are busy people, sort out your domestic affairs and leave us free to go after the true criminals.'

Sergeant Stoute had been in the police for years, he knew all the stories. You can't get to officer level in SVG without the songs and tales, and he didn't let the force down that evening. We heard about the man who sold and stole the same pig five times in one night, he told us about the policewoman who handcuffed a jumbie one Sunday and couldn't explain the empty cell Monday morning. Corporal Willis Feetlock, traffic officer by day, Miss Synthia Denning at night? We found out about him too.

Joel and Stoute gave us all ten verses of 'Go home to your wife, Mr Fife', I wondered where my husband met 'Mrs Shallow, the woman who didn't like to follow'. After an hour, Stoute picked up his trombone and played a delighted Gabrielle 'Happy Birthday'. A long wail of the instrument was the signal to leave.

As we packed our bags we realised he wasn't quite finished with Estelle.

'Young lady,' he said. 'I'm letting you off this evening, the Chief of Police won't approve, so I have to set a condition.'

Estelle stared lovingly at him. 'What is it?' she asked.

'That you drive me home.'

Estelle curtseyed. 'Thank you, Inspector, I can do that.'

Trombone under his left arm, Stoute saluted Joel. 'Good evening Sergeant Providence.' He turned to me and bowed. 'Mrs Providence.'

He gave a nod to my father, another to Shirley, and kissed Gabrielle on the cheek. One stumbling, the other tall and erect, he and Estelle made for his car.

My father went with Gabrielle and Shirley, and me and Joel were left staring at each other, thankful that the case was closed.

But we didn't stare for long. We had the house to ourselves, our suffering would soon be over.

cassie and the mason murder

My service in the police force had me all over SVG. Tiny dots on the blue maps in every station wall turned into dusty villages or rowdy towns, no Geography lesson could touch mixing and mingling. The Grenadine islands my father took me to at Easter and Christmas as a child sprinkled their magic over me once more when on patrol.

Sometime in my early teens, I used to dream about a female giant as tall as the coconut tree in our yard which bombed the house during hurricane season. The coconut heart was her head, the green or dry branches her straggling locks. The giant would set out from Grenada and stomp! Carriacou, stomp! Mayreau, stomp! Mustique. One Grenadine island then another, thirteen huge strides, and she was on mainland SVG. What could I do but laugh at my childishness when on duty in Union Island or Canouan?

Corporal or constable, I can't remember a single day when I cursed the job. No matter how late I staggered home, or how battered, by morning I was ready to go again. Police work was my vocation, no earthly currency could measure it. All hell broke loose one morning when Sylvia Peppy from Largo Heights broke three fingernails apprehending a thief, a crease in her blouse and you would think the end was nigh. Simmer,

Sylvia, I used to beg her, let the uniform do the work, keep dressing up for the weekend shows.

The Mulraines are not big-grain people, but after seven months of combat training, I could hold off any man who wasn't a giant. Those women who called me 'sister' then lashed out to scrawl my face, same block-then-tackle for them. Promotion to corporal and a taste of detective work in Kingstown only increased my liking for policing. Before I met my husband I gambled and spent my wages on myself, the force met the rest of my needs.

Once I slipped on the navy-blue trousers and crisp grey blouse, I didn't want to hear that blood was thicker than water. Money? Liquor? Wrong woman. Junior officers did most of the 'domestic' work at the station, but every now and again there would be a murder, and the police station would spring into life. Proper detective stuff at last!

I remember my first murder, a sudden death in Paul's Avenue. A shopkeeper, face down, the muscles of his back melting under the early-morning sun one Saturday. No injuries, no medical conditions, no witnesses. How could a six-footer collapse just like that? And when he was in the ground before his soul could depart his body, who wouldn't feel sorry for his tearful wife?

Detectives interviewed the dead man's widow, his family, friends and neighbours. Shopkeepers too, and vendors from the nearby market. But their notebooks came back near empty. If they got two pages between them that was plenty. Resting our feet at the station after another day knocking at doors, we would laugh like the lunatics who pepper Bay Street on pay day: scores of Vincentians who didn't *see* anything, or *hear* anything: we would have to sign them up to make a record!

But you can only laugh so much. When the investigation

rolled into month two, I began to consider what we were missing.

I got brave. Please let me join the detective squad proper, I begged Sergeant De Freitas one evening when we were alone, there was something I would like to try out. Her eyes went south, north, then south again. Knowing her reputation, she could have been searching for determination in my face, she might have been measuring my hips. 'All right, Mulraine,' she said, 'do what you have to, but don't be the woman to let me down.' I can't remember a sweeter nod from an officer.

Me and Miss Largo Heights got busy. Sylvia liked to dress up, and I didn't mind a little disguise myself. A short-sighted old lady in a peach spinster frock, her stepsister in matching blue, that was us drinking mauby and eating stale cakes in Paul's Avenue soon after. The residents looked dry-up, rough, they would argue over the colour of a green bottle. We flashed a little cash, we listened, we prodded and poked. In the evening we went again, broke up arguments, and bought drinks to calm everyone down. It was miles tougher than regular police work. 'Check for poison,' an old woman eventually let slip when we upgraded her malt to Guinness, 'some widows deadlier than a spider.'

Team-play, patience and stamina were part of the job, I found out during that spell as a 'junior' detective. If you can't get your evidence *this* way, you have to try *that* one. But above all, patience; no rush, things in their own time. I was to learn that hard lesson when I took on the case of a man from Mesopotamia, my first murder as a PI.

Gus Kenkede was twenty-six, but when he had in liquor he could easily pass for a man in his forties. He was single, not bad-looking, with a gentle face and tight curly hair. 'His woman run off with this builder from Firebun,' people sniggered when he rolled up in Mespo one Sunday morning.

'Poor Gus, he look so meek and mild, he must be one of those fellas who bad-lucked with women.'

In SVG you could meet a friend in Chauncey on Monday, by Friday she might be living happy in Sans Souci on the opposite side of the island. People shift, they discover relatives far and wide. Had Gus come to Mespo to change his luck, or to find an uncle to ask a favour? No one ever found out, for Gus took his blows and kept his mouth shut. Out of pride or shame, he held on to his past. He was a man of secrets, a batsman happy to build his innings with singles and twos.

Rumours and teasing he could ignore, but drink was a different matter. And unfortunately, he couldn't hold his share of liquor. Rum and beer were beginning to shrivel his body, he was going downhill faster than his bike. When the men played cards or dominoes he would draw up a stool, looking on, but out of the noisy circle. He was happy to set up late with them, but where they had a cool bed and a hot lover waiting, it was always home alone to the radio, a paperback novel or a cricket magazine.

Every Sunday morning Gus washed and polished his bicycle. Lovingly, carefully, for the bike was his living. He delivered fresh bread from the Reddock bakery to the shops on the *Rayleigh*, you didn't have to get up early to hear the tinkling of his bell.

He was quiet, and with a generous side. If you were tired, he would let you sling your shopping onto the handlebar of his bike and drop it off at your house. When the wind got up during September, he would carry your child to school for a dollar; if you couldn't pay, he would take a Julie mango or a fat yam instead. My husband was one of the few men who knew him reasonably well, and he was the reason I took on the case.

Phillip Mason was born in Petit Bordel, but moved to Mespo in his teens. A handsome ladies' man, the businessman was going through a divorce at the time, his wife holding out for half of everything, and the banks losing patience with him. One Sunday there was a fete in a village two miles from Mespo, and the two men clashed.

It was a good dance, with sweet music and tasty food. A local band was playing, they were giving away the drinks at the price. Some of the ravers saw Gus and Mason leave the hall arguing around midnight. Gus chucked Mason in the chest, once, twice, and twice more. Taller and stronger, Mason grabbed Gus by the wrist and forced him down on the bonnet of a car before he could get to five.

Pushing and shoving is no big deal at a dance in SVG. People get high and behave foolish, drink and sweet music can be a fatal brew. But when a woman rolled up that night, ears pricked up, and eyes began to tear. Because it was Indra Greaves.

Indra was thirty-one, and so beautiful, the men in the district felt a pain in the belly just watching her stroll to post a letter. A seamstress with hypnotic brown eyes, she had twisted and perfumed her short black hair for the fete. Men had to lock their eyes, women hung their heads in salute.

Gus was a sharp dresser, and the luck was running with him that night. For every dance Indra gave Mason, she put aside one for him. Gus, the poor fella who could only afford a bike! Someone told Indra about the scuffle outside, so she gave a friend her brandy and went to separate them, pulling Mason off Gus.

'I don't want no man fighting over me. Sort out your nonsense and don't poison my name!'

The two men staggered back into the hall after that. Moments later, a woman thought she saw Indra speed off like a cook remembering a pot on the stove.

The fete was mellow in the early hours, no fussing, no more incidents. Nothing to interrupt the flow of sweet calypso, reggae and soul. When the music shut down at three the revellers drifted home. A couple of hours later, a nurse racing to catch an early van to Kingstown found Mason's body by the roadside.

The solution to the murder was obvious to everyone on latitude 13 degrees north, longitude 61 degrees west. Girl, boy, woman and man in SVG were investigators now. On the beach, at the roadside, in the shops, I could hear them sniggering. Why was I bothering to defend a man who was ninety-nine percent guilty, and the other one percent already swinging from the gallows? Like children learning to count backwards from ten to one, the new detectives recited the facts of the murder to me on their fingers.

Gus and Mason got into a quarrel at the dance; they were swapping blows by the front door; Indra went out to part them; the men went back into the hall; hours later, just off the main road from Mespo to Peruvian Vale, someone strangled Mason, leaving his body at the edge of the road.

The bare facts didn't make sense to me. Who but a fool would commit a crime knowing full well he would be the chief suspect? Phillip Mason was thirty-nine, five-eleven and lean. The sorry-looking corpse in the police pictures didn't resemble the businessman who ran a supermarket in Belair and owned two fishing boats. He was wearing a white shirt and black trousers, was this a man on the way home from a spree, with music still in his body, and love on his mind?

No look of surprise on the face, no final desperate plea to his attacker for mercy. I was to study the photographs till my eyes hurt. My magnifying glass zoomed in and out over the swelling and the weals left by the cord that did the fatal damage. Mason was strong, yet there were no marks on his hands to show that he tried to defend himself. Did he know his attacker, or was he caught totally off guard?

Joel went with me to the local police station to see Gus. 'Get Cassie,' Gus had sent word to him, 'tell her don't worry about fees.'

If the station wasn't the most basic on the mainland or down the Grenadines, then good luck to the winner of the trophy. A desk, a map, a radio, a bookcase, three chairs and an unsteady wooden table under two empty bowls and a small chocolate cake, Joel could only shake his head at the sight. Burly Sergeant Fox pulled open the rusty cell door, let Gus out and said, 'Just going to the shop across the road to get some plates, Providences. If the three of you finish before I get back, make sure you shut the station door.'

He drew a white flannel from his trouser pocket, wiped his forehead, and we watched him roll off into the darkness.

The station was a sight to behold and Gus wasn't much better. He was still wearing the clothes from the dance, a lilac shirt and grey trousers reeking of old sweat, liquor, the damp cell, and stale perfume. He stank of urine, the station of mouldy socks and a peppery soup, he looked like a man in danger of renting out control of his life to the first taker.

'I didn't kill Mason, you know,' Gus said as soon as we had all taken a chair. 'It wasn't me.'

Two years in the district, and this was the first time I had heard him say more than 'Hello'. He had an unusually soft voice, almost like an altar boy.

'You didn't?' I said.

'No.'

'Who killed him then?'

'I can't tell you that.'

'Half the crowd saw you and Mason arguing,' I pointed out, 'you pushed him in the chest, and he had you up against a car.'

Gus shrugged. 'So what? Plenty of men jostle when they go to a dance: what's wrong with that?'

'Nothing,' I said, for he didn't seem to appreciate the sentence a guilty verdict would land him. 'So long as one of them doesn't commit murder.'

'Well I'm not the murderer.'

The soft voice pleaded, his tight body begged me to believe him.

'What was the scuffle about?' I asked.

'I can't remember,' he mumbled. 'I had in too much drink.'

'Did you?'

'Yes.'

'So you don't remember a woman separating the two of you either?'

Gus looked across at me as if the question had helped to kick-start his memory. 'You mean Indra?'

'Yes.'

'Ah, she was just "breasting" herself as usual.'

I placed the notebook on the table. When he realised that I wasn't going to put another question he knew what he had to do.

'You know Indra,' he continued. 'She has to "front up" herself when there's a crowd. First she want to dance with you, then she change her mind. Next moment she taking your hand and embracing you so you know that *she* running things, not you.'

'So that's what the fight was about, was it?

Gus frowned. 'Fight? Who was fighting?'

'You and Mason.'

'That wasn't a fight, that was just a bit of push-and-shove.'

'The fight was later then, when Mason was walking home?'

'I told you, Mrs Providence, I didn't kill Mason. I didn't see him again after we went back into the hall.'

'You didn't go looking for him?'

'No.'

117

'He didn't come looking for you to finish things?'

'No.'

'So you both danced the night away after the squabble?'

'You could call it that.'

'What time did you leave?'

'Late.'

'How late?'

'An hour before the end.'

'Any particular reason?'

'I had to catch some sleep to get ready for my deliveries.'

'Who did you go home with?'

Gus hesitated. And I hoped he could see now that without an alibi, he might end up in a stinking cell in Kingstown with three hefty men rubbing their hands and waiting for his eyelids to begin to droop so they could sing him a lullaby.

'Nobody.' His voice died away like the last drop from a bottle of fizzy water. 'Couple of fellas from my area were outside the hall laughing and joking, but they don't have a job to go to. I had to get home to sober up.'

'Which way did you go?'

'I took a shortcut through the banana field.'

I held back a sigh. Did he truly want to bag himself a life sentence?

'And what happened when you got home?' I asked.

Gus looked at me as if I was either naive or foolish, or both. He said, 'What do men do at the end of a dance?'

'I don't know,' I replied. 'Tell me.'

'They go to sleep, Mrs Providence. If they don't have a woman to entertain, they open the window to let in some cool sea breeze, and go to bed hugging their pillow.'

'Really?' I said, for the reply surprised me. But its importance didn't strike me at the time.

'So what do you think happened to Mason?' Joel asked,

and I could tell that he didn't think we were going to get much more from this visit.

'Mason's running a business, Mr Providence,' Gus answered, 'he's popular. If he didn't walk home with his friends, he wouldn't have trouble digging up a woman to take home to cool his bed.'

'Indra?' I asked.

Gus thought about it for a while. 'Na,' he said eventually. 'Indra was too flirty-flirty that night. Asking me to partner her, then, just when things getting romantic between us, wheeling into his arms to finish the tune with him. The next record strutting with him to start, and ending the set with me. Mason was so vex when she was "closing in" on me during a Percy Sledge soft tune, no way he was going to bother with her after that.'

'You're sure?' I put it to him.

'Yes. Indra had him so mad he was almost spitting fire.'

'And after the scuffle you didn't bother with her again?'

'No, Mrs Providence,' Gus answered with a sureness that seemed strange coming from this quiet man. 'I have good dancing feet, you think I would spend my night worrying about Indra when east-west-north-south I could reach out and groove another sexy partner?'

'My goodness,' I thought, 'a new Gus: what have I let myself in for?'

I stared at the soft boyish face he would soon lose if he carried on drinking. I saw the black eyes dart from me to Joel and back, pleading for help, but trying to appear brave and macho. Petty thieves went mad in a cell of two, did he know what happened in the early hours in a jail in Kingstown when men six were banged up together in a three-by-four-by-five space with a single pillow between them?

Then, just like that, Gus began to sob.

'Me and Mason had a little scramble but I didn't kill him,' he cried, his tears and spit dripping on the table separating us. 'Tell her Joel. Tell Cassie I don't have murder in me.'

Joel patted him on the shoulder then hugged him. 'Rise up Gus man, we'll find the murderer.'

We let him sob, his head buried in his hands, his back convulsing. A few minutes like this then he stopped, his eyes red, his shoulders slack now. He pushed the chair back and dragged himself up like a man who had scored more defeats than wins in his short life. We got up too, and watched him make to return to the cell. A couple of paces in his journey, I noticed a dip in his walk.

'What's wrong with your leg?' I asked.

'Nothing,' he mumbled without looking back.

'The injury,' I said. 'Mason?'

'I fell off my bike.'

He went into the cell, closed the door, and picked up a magazine.

'Let's go and see Indra,' Joel suggested as we were walking home, 'she's the key witness.'

But I wasn't sure. 'Nah,' I told him. 'Too early. All we have to put to her is what Gus told us. We have to hit her with something tougher.'

'But she might catch a plane out.'

'And let down her customers? And tell the world she was guilty times ten?'

The Saturday after the robbery in Vermont, a newspaper invited me for an interview. In the next run it published photos of me with the Jeffersons outside the gallery in Kingstown. Big mistake. I had to turn down offers for security work, it seemed like every engaged couple in SVG wanted me to keep an eye on their other half. From leeward to windward, drunks offered me tips on trapping criminals, every dog and cat was now an expert in the art of crime and deduction. This murder made things ten times worse. I couldn't walk a mile without some donkey taking me by the elbow and giving me their account of what happened that night. Please, I begged one and all, it's a police case, wait for the trial.

But you can't stop some people. What Vincies don't know they have no problem inventing. I had to stay indoors to escape the braying, I lost my appetite, my legs became sore and painful. Leave me alone, I felt like screaming out loud, what's the matter with you blasted fools?

Joel played me my Fatty Dan CDs and massaged my shoulders, what would I do without my husband? He smoothed away the wrinkles on the brow of the old woman he woke up with now, when he saw me dip, he reassured me with his arms. Did I take on too much? Was it too soon to tackle a murder?

Gus was his friend so Joel offered to help out with a bit of digging. The old faithful, mix and mingle. Straight after work each day he drove to listen to the talk in the rum shops and bars in the region. He splashed out on cakes, plantain chips and free drinks, and made notes with his eyes and ears. Anyone dropping by the Providences deep in the night would have found an old fisherwoman and her husband sifting their crayfish basket of evidence.

Night after night Joel went out, but the catch didn't come to much. It was more silvery sprats than blue tuna. The three pages in my notebook from the morning of the murder were only up to a miserable five a week later. Each suspect on the whiteboard had ticks and crosses balanced out.

'What now Cassie?' Joel asked on Saturday afternoon as we were soaking up the breeze in the porch.

He was trying to help, I knew, but *I* was the investigator. Sooner or later I had to face my tormentors.

'Who did Gus go to the dance with?' I asked him.

'Hezzie, Tornelle and Sagga,' he replied. 'That's his crowd.'

'Let's hear what they have to say.'

Hezzie was thirty-seven, short, stumpy and bow-legged. Thick forearms told you what he did to support his family. The farmer was taking his supper in the porch when I went to see him, just after five that evening. He pointed to a wooden stool, then raised an enamel bowl of soup to his mouth with both hands.

'What you want to know?' he asked, resting the bowl on the floor.

'What you remember about the dance.'

'What exactly?'

'Anything you can tell me.'

Hezzie licked the corners of his mouth with a thick red tongue.

'My best memory was Gus grooving Indra, "soft-tuning" her to Percy Sledge,' he said. 'So close air couldn't get through. Ripe, I tell you. Mason was standing watching them with this jealous, vex look. Ripe, I tell you. But poor Gus, fancy trying to play in the Indra league.'

'Which one is that?'

'The "high life" division. Indra don't mix with you unless you have rating.'

'No?'

'Let me put it this way, Cassie: if you can't cash up for Hadaway dresses and French perfume, no second look for you. Cognac not on the menu? Don't think you can fob her off with a malt. Wrong woman.'

I couldn't follow him. 'So why did she ask Gus to dance?' I asked. 'Why pick him from all the lavettes that night? If Indra is a glamour-girl, how come she was favouring Gus the pauper?'

Hezzie grinned. 'I was up quarter-night wondering that,' he said, 'and then it hit me.'

'What?'

'The reason she picked Gus.'

'To get at Mason?'

'Na, Indra too smart for that.'

'Smart?'

'Yes, clever. Plenty clever. Ripe, I tell you.'

'Taking up with the quietest man in the district? The man with nothing?'

Hezzie brought up an ugly laugh in tune with a belch. 'You don't know how to measure her either.'

He laughed again, louder this time, and I felt a fool.

'Then tell me how, Hezzie,' I begged. 'Lend me the scale.'

'No scale, Cassie. The quarrel between Gus and Mason didn't involve Indra.'

I dragged my chair closer to him and the bowl. 'No?' I said.

'No.' Hezzie looked around to see what else he could find to eat. 'One Saturday some time back, Mason was driving home tight, and he knocked Gus off his bike by the bridge. He promised him $1000 not to go to the police because that was his second accident of the year. Up to a fortnight ago how much you think Gus receive? Seven hundred? Six? No. Four hundred dollars. Gus was bugging him to pay up, that's what they were fighting over: Indra was just a side dish. Ripe, I tell you.'

I thanked Hezzie and left. Some things made sense now, but just as many lined up on the confused side. I thought of going back to Gus, but my mind still said, 'Wait, check Tornelle and Sagga. Better to hear more about the spree, best to get their news on the accident.'

Tornelle was a slim man with at least five creases on a narrow sloping forehead. His wife, Donna, was twice his width, and without a single line. They didn't add much to Hezzie's account.

'The supermarket in trouble,' Tornelle said, when I stopped making notes. 'Mason could barely raise $400 to pay Gus.'

'And Indra?' I asked.

Donna got in before her husband could answer. 'Indra was only the salad between Gus and Mason. She was just trying to sweeten Gus up so he would hold off Mason for a few months. If Gus was sharpening his cutlass, no way he was going to tidy Indra's garden. She might tease you and flirt, but no man but Mason ever take her over the line. Take it from me.'

Theresa Durant was thirty, with a narrow face, big round eyes, and a young afro. She opened the door to Sagga's house, my final stop that evening. When I asked her for Sagga she replied, 'You mean the man I used to have? The one who dropped me to pick up a blue $10 note?'

I couldn't read this delivery, so I let it pass by.

'Is he home?' I asked again.

'No. Out on a fare,' she said. 'Short trip, shouldn't be long.'

Ten minutes later, when still no sign of Sagga, Theresa asked if she could help.

'Were you at the dance?' I asked.

'You mean the night they murdered Mason?'

'Yes.'

'Yes, I was there.'

'What kind of night was it?'

'Good. Ripe. Poor Gus.'

'Poor Gus?'

'Yes,' she repeated, 'poor man.'

'Mason is the man you should be sorry for.'

'I feel for him, yes, but I can't believe Gus did it.'

'Why not?'

'Because Gus doesn't have murder in him.'

Boxes, books, cups, car spares, clothes, electronic gadgets

and bottles of drink cluttered the room. It was a mess of a place. We were at the tiny dining table, I drew my chair closer to hers.

'You know him well, then?'

'Enough to know what he wouldn't do.'

'So better than most people?'

'The little I know satisfy me.'

'You will vouch for him?'

'I can only tell it as I see it.'

'When did the two of you get friendly?'

Theresa glanced nervously at her mobile on the table. Then she went to the front door, put a fat key in it, and locked it.

'Look Cassie,' she said when she returned. 'What I have to say is very delicate. I know you have your job to do, but this is my life. Me and Sagga used to be engaged, but things not really working out. *He* knows that, *I* know that. But we don't want our inside troubles out on the street and in the mouths of the newsmongers.'

I nodded to remind her that I earned my living keeping secrets as well as easing them out. 'I understand,' I assured her.

She called Sagga's mobile. No answer. She sighed. 'Another fare.'

I could see that my work was trespassing on her life so I asked her, 'You're sure you want to carry on?'

Theresa closed her eyes as if weighing things up. 'Yes,' she said eventually.

'When you're ready then.'

'Near the end of the fete,' Theresa said in a soft voice, 'Sagga told me he had a fare to Kingstown. "Short trip," he said, "back soon." But I know Sagga, money is his queen. Another fare would spring up after town, then a third, and I would be sitting waiting on a tree stump when he roll in at six. I was giving Gus a friendly dance when Sagga tapped me on the shoulder and said his passenger was ready. Go home with Gus, he said, he would pick me up there in forty-five minutes.'

Theresa paused and took a deep breath. I gave her time.

'A fare.' She forced a laugh, the kind that touches your soul. 'Who would put a taxi fare above their beloved, especially after a sweet night out?'

I patted her on the right shoulder and rubbed it gently.

'So me and Gus set out for home,' she picked up her account after the rub.

'What time was this?'

'2.39.'

'How come you remember the exact time?'

'Sagga checked his mobile. He promised to collect me from Gus 3.30 at the latest.'

'Fair enough.'

'Anyway, me and Gus knew the shortcut was dark, but we decided to take a chance. We stumbled and fell over so much, when we got to his house I could truly use a drink. Looking from the road you wouldn't believe it, but Gus has a proper little mansion there, you know. Bookcase, music centre, pine wardrobe, leather settee. And a king-size bed.'

'What did you have to drink?' I asked, for I didn't want to believe where her conversation was leading.

'*Captain Bligh* XO: smooth rum, real smooth.'

'And Gus?'

'A juice. He had to go to work in a couple of hours.'

'And after the drinks?'

'We talked. I felt easy with him, Gus is a good listener for a man. His time in Firebun, my spell with my father in Mount Bentick, we didn't hold back anything. Was it true Sagga was saving up to go to Trinidad to buy a new taxicab? Was a fact, not rumour, I put Gus right: when my beloved had his fleet of taxis, it was goodbye Theresa. After this Gus put on some music and asked me to dance. Not loud, but enough volume to get in a good set.'

'And a second set?'

'That's what Gus wanted. But his body was so hot, and I was a little merry, you know how if you're not careful you can let that early-morning devil sweep your woman-sense away.'

'Yes,' I said, no use denying it.

'Twins I could probably manage, I joked with him, but I wasn't sure I could handle the triplets he was going to hit me with the mood he was in. And do you know what Cassie? We burst out laughing like two naughty children.'

'And when you stopped laughing?'

'Leave Sagga, Gus begged me, he would take care of me. When Sagga got the money together and bought his plane ticket to Trinidad, he wanted me to tell him it was over. Then he kissed me on the cheek and walked me home.'

'What time did you leave his house?'

'3.57. I phoned Sagga and left a message to say not to bother to pick me up.'

'Anything unusual on the way?'

'No. It was dark, you couldn't see much.'

'How was Gus then?'

'Zinging. Happy. He asked if he could hold my hand, and I let him. Why not? "Theresa girl," I said to myself, "if Sagga doesn't want you, this man might." He has love in him, Gus, and I believe I have love in me too.'

'And you still feel that way?'

'Even more now. I would do anything I could to help him.'

'Even lie?'

Theresa shook her head. 'No, I wouldn't do that.'

'And if they find him guilty?'

Theresa didn't pause, didn't draw breath. 'I will visit him in jail and support him until they find the real killer. When he was walking me home, we went past Mason's house and he told me Mason knocked him off his bike some time back. Mason promised him $1000, but was sticking at 400. Gus needs someone to care for him. To make him stand up for what is his.'

'How did he seem then?'

'He was mad. Who wouldn't be?'

My heart sank.

'There was this car parked by the house,' Theresa continued, 'he was furious because Mason had a new vehicle but still refused to pay up.'

'What make was the car?' I asked.

'I couldn't really see it properly. It was brown or yellow, one of those colours.'

By now it was after seven, Joel would be worrying about me, it was time to get home.

'Did you have your mobile with you that night, Theresa?' I asked.

'Yes. I have it on all the time. Customers want a taxi round the clock these days.'

'Took any photos?'

'A few.'

She reached for the phone from the table. There were pictures of her, Sagga, Indra, Tornelle and Gus, and shots of the crowd, wild, merry. Mason was there too – in the early snaps – in an orange shirt and tight white trousers, grinning, posing, with only a few hours of life left in him.

'Thanks Theresa,' I said, as I got up to go. 'Hope things work out.'

When I got home Joel was playing his steelpan. He put away the sticks and went to share out our supper. As I ate the fried plantain, I went through my notes with him.

'You're getting close to docking in the harbour then?' he said.

'You could call it that,' I replied, a little hesitant.

'Why the fret then,' he asked, 'why you frowning so hard?'

'Gus didn't tell us the truth,' I explained. 'Where did he go after walking Theresa home? He was mad when he saw Mason's new vehicle, why not ambush the man who owed him money? If someone had you up against a car and you caught him "tight" and alone in the dark, wouldn't you take your revenge?'

Whenever things are hotting up my head, the Caribbean Sea is there for me with a sweet breeze. And, thankfully, Joel can suss when to let me rest. I was back into my stride as a PI, but it was time to put the case away for the day. I climbed into my hammock at the back of the house and closed my eyes. Joel massaged my shoulders, rubbing out the knots. Then he played with my toes, stroking, rubbing, gently tugging them. In no time I was asleep.

As usual our neighbour woke up the district early on Sunday, playing her hymns at full volume for all to hear. I made bakes for breakfast, and scrambled eggs with chives and garlic, while Joel pleaded with her to turn the music down. We were in the yard feeding our chickens their rice at eleven when Mother Reddock stopped by. The number one baker in the district, she was on the way to the Spiritual Baptist church, in a rich maroon robe crowned with a blue headtie. She looked splendid and spiritual.

'Morning Mr and Mrs Providence,' she hollered in her loud church voice, as if we were in the back row of the congregation, and deaf to go with it. 'You two busy?'

'No,' we said at the same time.

'Can you spare five minutes?'

Mother Reddock was sixty, a short square-shaped woman with squeezed-in eyes and fat cheeks in a contented face. She was always chirpy, like one of those women who had reserved a place 'on high', and had it confirmed. We went inside to the front room.

'A glass of mauby?' Joel asked.

The Mother grinned like a teenage girl anxious to try something her mother warned her against.

'Got anything with a touch more power?'

'Beer?'

'Mightier?'

Joel fetched a bottle of rum. She poured herself a shot, and sniffed it like a connoisseur.

'It's to do with Gus,' she said, after a sip.

'What about him?' I asked, as she chased the rum with cold water.

'He's a decent young fellow.'

'What, reliable and honest?'

'Yes. But more than that.'

Joel got a beer and sat down with us at the table, as if he felt something big was coming.

Mother Reddock took out an exercise book from the middle of her bible. 'This is the bakery log,' she explained. 'You can see what time Gus came to work that terrible and dreadful morning.'

I flicked through the pages until I found the date of the murder. '6.42.' I pointed to the entry. 'And 6.47 the day before.'

'In two years, he hasn't been late once.'

'And he behaved the same the morning of the murder?' Joel asked.

'Not a grain of difference.'

'Can I borrow the book?' I asked.

'Sorry.' Mother Reddock put out her hand for it. 'I will have to get you a copy. Gus is very particular, he says the bakery log is our life. The yeast we use, the amount of flour, the oven temperature, which shopkeepers didn't take their quota, we record everything.'

Joel looked puzzled, and he wasn't the only one.

'Why,' I asked, 'what's it to do with him?'

Mother Reddock took another drink of water.

'Gus owns half the bakery, Cassie,' she said. 'Nine months ago it was a cross keeping it going, so I warned him he might have to look for another work. The following afternoon he put an envelope with four thousand dollars on the table. I don't know where he got the money, you have to know when to ask and when to let questions die. The business is in three names now, same two bakers, same Gus delivering.'

Was this good news or bad? I was tempted to take the Monday off to wipe the whiteboard in my office clean. Hezzie, Tornelle, Donna, Theresa, and now Mother Reddock were behind Gus, did Sagga back him too?

The next morning I drove round to Sagga's house to see what could he add about the night. It was just after eight, and he was polishing his Datsun taxi. Sagga was forty, and a hearty eater if his stomach didn't lie. As I watched him shine the vehicle, I thought of the choice Theresa might soon have to make: between one man mending a bike, and the other, a flashy car.

'Cassie.' Sagga sounded as bright as the morning. 'How things?'

'So-so,' I answered glumly.

'Any luck with the Mason business?'

'Things rolling slow.'

'Hope you track the killers down soon, people getting all jittery.'

'Don't worry,' I said. 'I've booked the best suite in the jail in Kingstown for the murderer.'

'How's fat Fox at the station getting on with his investigation?'

'Sergeant Fox is halfway through interviewing the dance crowd – same as me.'

As I was about to ask for a slot with him, Sagga held up a hand. Seconds later he was in the driver's seat taking a call.

'Just finish shining her,' he said, obviously to a customer. 'Pick you up in fifteen minutes?'

His mobile must have been on *Vibrate*, I was sure I didn't hear it ring. But when you got that many calls seemed only fair to have the phone on *Low*.

'Business?' I said, when he climbed out the car.

He looked as happy as Happy Fraser. 'A client. I can't get a rest for these people.'

'Can I come by later?' I asked.

'Come anytime, Cassie. You know me, always home.'

As Sagga was driving off to add another twenty dollars to his fortune, my mind ran on Indra. Was she at home crying for Mason? Didn't matter. Was time to pay her a visit. But not directly.

Indra lived in a large house close to the main road. Lovely white and light-blue building, simple design. Customers approached the house from the back where she did her sewing. In the two days I was watching her, Indra only left the house once – to collect a parcel from the post office. In the shop across the road, I flicked through pictures from the fateful night with the drinkers and those who took to lime-ing at any bar or shop where there was a new face. Putting the mobile snaps together got me the same story: a happy crowd sweating, grinning, dancing, no Mason after midnight.

The next day I drove to Belair. Who else knew Mason? Did he have any business rivals or enemies? His youngest daughter was running the supermarket now, a tall, solid young woman with a forbidding look. Her voice was deep and sad.

'Hard to say how long the store will last,' she said. 'Dad

sold the Nissan, and now we have to sell the speedboat to hold off the bank. Things tough like hell. My father had his bad ways but he was a good man. He didn't deserve to leave earth that way.'

So how to explain the car outside Mason's house that night? Theresa was a little tipsy on drink and promises, but so high to imagine a car? And if Mason didn't have a vehicle, whose car was in his yard?

Indra set off for Kingstown on the Friday, business day, in a Honda. She was sharp on the gas, my car rattled on the flat and nearly died uphill trying to keep up with her. At Diamond she turned off the main road and pulled in at an unpainted concrete building. Ten minutes later she came out and crossed the road to the bus stop with a brown briefcase. She hailed the next van to the capital, and climbed in next to the driver as important women always do in SVG, to keep the pleats in their skirt.

Funny how you can drive past a building a hundred times and not really notice it. When I stepped in now, my first guess was that it was a garage. Tall breadfruit, mango and plum trees in the front yard looked down on eight vehicles – four cars, a jeep and three motorbikes. A dread with thick locks down to his lap was sprawling in a wicker chair in the reception. He was taking his breakfast of coffee and spliff.

'Morning,' I called out.

'Hail Miss,' the dread drawled. 'Which vehicle you after?'

'A car with a nice price,' I replied, thankful for his help.

He took me to the backyard. There, under a plum tree, the Honda was cooling down.

'That car can go, man,' I said. 'The lady who was just in here, she was giving it a really good run.'

The dread gave me a nasty look. 'You police or something?'

I answered him with a cute smile. 'Me? Nah.'

He took a long draw to settle that. 'Well, police or civilian, lady, this business is legitimate. You have a clean driving licence and full insurance? No worries. You don't? Try a different hire company.'

'Thanks dread,' I said, 'get her ready for me for tomorrow.'

'Pleasure, Miss.'

Sooner or later, in any small Caribbean country, two healthy people are bound to meet. That Sunday afternoon, I decided to go for a swim in the river near where we live. I was searching for somewhere to rest my bag when I glanced a figure to my right.

Drying her hair with care, Indra was sitting on a large flat stone, her eyes closed, her legs stretched out. She was wearing a two-piece chocolate-brown swim suit, the lower half like short shorts. She had a fresh, black face, with a soft, well-made chin. Her breasts were small and shapely. Her stomach had a gentle smooth curve; if I was a man catching her like this, I would beg to dry her, cry even, and take my sweet time with the towel.

She opened her eyes, slowly, when she heard me trying not to disturb her. And, for a moment, we stared at one another like two lovers who have fallen out but are too stubborn to apologise.

'Cassie,' her soft voice broke the silence.

'Yes?' I answered.

'You followed me down here, didn't you?'

I couldn't help a chuckle. 'What happened, you're the only woman who likes to cool off on a Sunday?'

'No, but I hear you've been watching me.'

'Me?' I said.

'Yes, you. You were by the shop opposite my house pretending you were drinking stout.'

'Who told you that story?'

'Cassie, look,' Indra said, 'I appreciate you have a job to do, but if you believe I had something to do with Phillip's murder, I hope you're woman enough to tell me so to my face.'

'Well, didn't you?' I said.

Indra got up, this woman with the gift of soft, glowing black skin and heavenly proportions. Seeing the wisps of soft black hair in a down line just below her navel, I could understand why men prayed to get close to her.

'No, Cassie, I could never do that,' she said.

'But you were with him on the night?'

'At the dance, yes.'

'And after?'

'I left before the end.'

'What time?'

'Just after midnight.'

'Why leave so early? The dance was mellow, why not stay and enjoy the jamboree?'

'Things were getting a little bit ugly. Every time I danced with Gus, Phillip wanted to make it three of us.'

'Why?'

'Gus is a boss dancer, Cassie. Phillip couldn't believe another man could find my rhythm so sweetly.'

'Gus is that good?'

'He is. And Phillip could spot it. *He* was always the man women queued up to groove with, and now Gus was stealing his glory: the same Gus everyone used to underrate.'

'So he got jealous, and fell into your trap?'

'It was just a little sport, a tight dance. I don't know why men get hot up over nothing!'

'That "Nothing" is probably why Mason is in his grave.'

Indra began to cry softly. She couldn't help the tears trickling down her face.

'Donna told me Phillip was planning to finish with me,'

she sobbed. 'Three years together, and he was threatening to walk away and leave me on my own!'

'So you decided to teach him a lesson?'

'Yes.'

'By killing him?'

Indra dabbed her eyes with the towel. 'No! I didn't kill him. I was trying to show him that someone else might want to take his place.'

'And it worked?'

'He was vex, yes.'

'Why did you pick Gus?'

'Phillip and Gus got into an accident, Cassie, and Phillip begged him not to go to the police. Soon after that his business got into trouble, so he couldn't pay Gus the amount he promised him. I was trying to get him to ease up on Phillip. Next thing I heard they were outside fighting.'

'And you went to separate them?'

'Yes.'

'And after they went back into the hall?'

'The quarrel upset me so I went home.'

I stepped closer to Indra. So close we were almost touching. I spoke directly into the beautiful face.

'Indra, if you can stand there and tell me such a bold-face lie on a Sunday, what's to stop you killing Mason?'

Indra came straight back with her answer, wrapped in a nervous laugh. 'What lie?'

'You didn't go home, you went by Mason.'

'Who told you that?' She sounded like a girl sleeping out for the first time trying to act brave on the journey home to face her parents.

'Indra,' I said softly, 'Mason went back into the hall after the fray, but then he vanished like a ghost. I checked hundreds of photos, and you can't find Mason in a single one. No mobile clicked him. But two people got *your* car speeding off with a passenger – the drinkers across the road from your house have the evidence.'

Indra eased away from me and sat down. She stretched out her legs and drew the towel up to her thighs. I sat beside her.

'I *did* drive Phillip home,' she said. 'For three years we were like man and wife, why shouldn't I?'

'You didn't just drive him home, you stayed by him.'

'Did I?' she said, and I could tell she was wondering what else the mobiles captured.

'Yes.'

'Who told you that?'

'Your car was outside his house.'

'What car?'

'The one you hired for the evening to impress him. To show him that your business was bringing in a good profit. A brown Honda, remember?'

'I didn't hire any car.'

'I snapped you two days ago Indra. And two witnesses saw the same car outside Mason's house.'

Indra was wearing a ring on her right fourth finger, she rubbed it subconsciously, and I felt for her.

'Yes,' she finally admitted. 'Yes, I was there. I wanted to let Phillip know that no man could ever take his place in my heart. I begged him to level with me. We could be a team, I told him, I was making good money now, I would pay off Gus if he would commit to me and make us official. I would help bail him out, we could become *partners* in every way.'

'Did he take up your offer?'

'Phillip is a proud man, Cassie, he wouldn't accept my help. "Let's wait till the supermarket is making a profit again, and we'll set a date." He promised me that. I had to beg him to take the six thousand in my brown bag to pay the bank. If things were switched round, he would do the same for me five times over, I had no doubt.'

'And after the promises?'

Indra turned to her left and looked at me, proudly, almost defiantly.

'We made love, Cassie. Slow and sweet and considerate and tender like the very first time. When you and your man fall out then make up, you know that bliss?'

'What time did you leave his place?' I asked, hearing the thin thing that called itself my voice.

'Four. Four-thirty? I don't know for certain. If that Sunday was a Saturday, Phillip wouldn't have to go to the supermarket, and we would stay in bed till evening. And he would still be alive. I apologised for trying to make him jealous, and gave him the money for Gus. He kissed me on my forehead and begged me to be patient. I could tell from his eyes he truly loved me. I wanted to drop him by the main road to get a van, but he said no. No hurry, he would take his time and walk. So I drove home and left him getting dressed.'

'Did you see anyone on the journey home?'

Indra gave me the kind of glare you would give a woman hanging out her washing in the middle of a downpour. 'That time of the morning?'

'Farmers off to the fields early, joggers, van drivers, people drifting home from the dance?'

'No. No one. Just Sagga: fancy waking up so early to scramble for fares.'

'What time was this?'

'I don't know, I was too full of sweet feelings to notice. You know that intense pleasure that lingers in your body for days when your man commit to you? Well it was like that. Then, just as I was slipping into a peaceful sleep, my neighbour was beating down my door telling me Phillip was dead.'

She was tearful in the middle of her answer, she began to weep now. I held her, and she locked her arms around my waist. A thought suddenly hit me when she unclasped her hands and began to dry her eyes: what happened to Mason's briefcase?

'How did I miss that?' I asked Joel when I got in.

'What?'

'The brown satchel Indra gave Mason. The police didn't mention it, if a farmer, passenger or runner strangled Mason, someone was bound to notice them with his case.'

'Perhaps the murderer hid it and came back for it during the night.'

'Or the murderer was driving.'

'Could be.'

'Sagga is back from Trinidad this weekend, I wonder if he saw anything: a strange face, someone in a hurry, a van driver up early to beat off rivals. Why don't we go and ask him?'

In SVG speculation about a murder could only last so long. Some nonsense about a tearful fish with a child's features was soon carrying the swing in the district. Then that went. Now, all the talk was about the new taxi Sagga had gone to Trinidad to buy.

Sagga's flight was due in at 6.30pm. He loved his food, *Immigration*, *Customs*, and a roadside stop for barbecued pork, would land him home by eight, Joel calculated. Tornelle and Hezzie were picking him up from the airport, why not go round to prick his memory?

I explained to Theresa that we were after a word with Sagga, there was a chance that he spotted something or someone. She seemed more anxious than usual, but she did her best to make us welcome. Linseed was her drink, and me and Joel never said no to that tonic. Sagga's crates, bottles, cardboard boxes, clothes and car spares were piled into one ugly corner, but the front room was tidier than on my previous visit. The linseed was running low when, going up to nine, we heard a vehicle rumble outside.

Theresa stepped out to greet Sagga, leaving me and Joel at the table. The moment she closed the front door I slipped into the bedroom.

In two-twos I was back with my husband listening to the conversation in the yard. Car talk from the men – the top speed of the vehicle, miles per gallon, wheel size – not much from Theresa. We could hear – if not see – Sagga passing round photos of the vehicle, I could imagine the men salivating. Once they had a picture to take home with them, the two friends left. I wondered how the reception would go.

'So Theresa, I'm back,' we heard Sagga say, now that they were alone in the porch.

'You get through?' Theresa asked.

'Yes. They shipping the taxi next week. Believe me, it was worth every dollar. It can take three passengers in the back and one in the front: that's the fashion and style in Trinidad.'

'Want something to eat?'

'You know me, I never say no.'

'I fixed you some chicken and rice.'

Travelling-bag in hand, Sagga staggered through the front door. When his eyes caught me and Joel, he pulled up suddenly.

'Good-good-good Evening,' he said, dragging his luggage past the door.

'We just dropped by to put our names down for the new vehicle,' I got in quickly to take away some of the surprise. 'The black cab could really take off.'

The mention of a booking, and he was himself again. He joined us at the table.

'A hit, a smash, first choice,' he said. 'Sagga Huggins going to change the way taxis run in SVG. Four passengers instead of one or two on a trip, profits will double-treble.'

'Your regulars will be queuing up for a spin,' Joel said.

'Fifteen signed up already.' Sagga tapped his right trouser pocket as if the passengers were in there fighting to be first. 'I'll add the two of you. Let me know when you're free.'

'Thanks, Sagga,' I said, 'but it will have to be after the case.'

'I thought that was over,' he said, keying in our names in his mobile.

'The police reckon it was a stranger in the district,' Joel explained. 'Probably one of those youngsters who go from place to place looking for someone to rob.'

'Same thing I was thinking,' he said. 'Ask Tornelle if I didn't tell him that.'

'Can I drop by tomorrow to check if you saw anything suspicious?' I said.

'Sorry, but I have an early drop to Kingstown.'

'How about now then?' I said. 'Shouldn't take long.'

'Fine,' he said, 'no worries.'

I put the question again. 'On the way home from your drop that Sunday, did you see anything or anyone unusual?'

'No.' Sagga was quite sure. 'The road was quiet all the way home. I didn't see a soul.'

'No drivers, no one going to the fields early? No cyclists, no runners up training before the morning heat?' Joel asked. 'No young man racing to beat rivals to the hills?'

Sagga thought for a while. 'No. The road was empty.'

'Mason was carrying a briefcase with some business papers,' I said, 'the police didn't find it.'

'Had to be the youngster, then,' Sagga suggested.

He got up suddenly, making a grunting, heaving noise.

'Excuse me,' he said. 'Bathroom.'

Going by the clock over the front door he was gone six minutes. We could hear noises coming from the bedroom, tumbling, clumping, rummaging. When Sagga came back he was rubbing his stomach and grimacing as if there was a knot in it.

'Food poisoning,' he explained. 'I had a beef roti at the airport, one bite and I could tell the damn thing was bad news.'

Still rubbing his stomach, he eased himself back into his chair.

'Some roti that,' Theresa said.

Sagga asked, 'What roti?'

'The one that made you confuse the bedroom and bathroom,' she explained.

Sagga couldn't follow her. 'Bedroom? Bathroom?'

I reached under my chair, pulled out a briefcase and dangled it in front of him.

'Recognise this?' I said.

A man noticing a bald patch for the first time might recoil a few inches, and that was Sagga now.

'No,' he stammered. 'What is it?'

'Mason's briefcase,' Joel said.

Sagga gave a little laugh. 'Why you showing me it?'

'He was carrying it on the day of the murder,' Theresa explained.

'So?' Sagga said.

'How did it end up in your bedroom?' I asked.

'Must be hundreds of briefcases like this in the country. They sell them in the market in town, you can get one from any vendor.'

I turned the case to show him. 'But this one has the initials *IG* on the back. Indra Greaves.'

'Then she's the murderer!'

'Sagga,' Theresa said in a gentle voice he might soon miss. 'Only adults here. Tell us the truth about that Sunday morning.'

Sagga dabbed away the sweat from his forehead. Sadness

took over his body, you could almost feel sorry for this important witness to the murder. He closed his eyes and quietly, almost in a whisper, he began.

'On the way home from my second fare, I saw Mason striding down the hill. I stopped. "You want me to drop you to work?" He shake his head. "Catching a van, I have a whole heap of things to think over." I could do you a good price, I say to him. Still no. Then I notice the briefcase, brown, fat. Had to be money in it, I could tell, plenty-plenty cash. Twenty times or more Indra ride to the bank in my taxi with it.

'Just then Mason put down the case by the side of the road so he could take a pee. I don't know what made me do it, I can't tell you the name of the devil possessing me. I truly liked the fellow. We used to talk good, Mason used to put business my way. How many times we share a beer and a souse?

'But I couldn't help myself. Not with the devil goading me. I grab this rope I always carry under the passenger seat, sling it round Mason neck, and begin to tighten it.

'He gurgle like a child, flap his hands, then sink to the ground. Because he wasn't expecting it, he didn't really struggle. My head was hot, itching, like there was a fire in it. Once I begin to tighten the rope I couldn't go back. When Mason stop breathing, I rolled him onto his belly. I didn't want to see his face, I didn't want him to see mine either. I catch a glimpse of the white bulging eyes, poor man, it was then I realised I truly strangled him. I tossed the briefcase onto the front seat and speed home. Thousands of dollars, what else could I do?'

Sagga opened his eyes and looked at each one of us in turn. He was what he was, only he knew inside how deep was his remorse.

Theresa went with me and Joel to the police station later that evening. The station was tidy and clean-smelling now, and brighter. Gus and Sergeant Fox were playing cards for matchsticks: Gus, ten sticks, the officer, one. We told them about Sagga's confession and showed them the brown case. Fox packed away the matches and covered his eyes in sadness.

'You would kill your friend for money?' the sergeant said, to himself, it seemed to me, not to us. 'So blatant you would take the life of someone in your community?'

None of us had an answer, for what could we say?

'We have to be better than that,' Fox said to our silence. 'Vincy people have to rise above greed, jealousy and pettiness. Four hundred years, we can't come this far together and give in to baseness.'

We nodded to this simple truth.

The sergeant offered Gus his hand. 'Good luck Gus man. Do what you have to.'

Gus looked fit. Even in the darkness of the evening you could see the shine to his eyes and the tone of his muscles. The cell had given him time to straighten himself, he looked like a new man.

'Cassie, Joel,' he said in his soft voice. 'Thanks, eh. I appreciate what you did for me. Come check me tomorrow, we'll settle fees and such.'

He took Theresa's hand, and they walked off together in the darkness. Joel took me by the waist and we set off for home too, silent, happy for Gus and Theresa, and saying a prayer for Mason.

cassie and the headmaster's problem

My husband's godson, Neville, was in Form 4 at Elma Francois Secondary school. He was a bright student, easy-going, too easy to influence. A form mate persuaded him to 'burn' Maths one Wednesday afternoon and, from then on, they were hailing a van to Rabacca when one of them could dig up some cash. If a pair of giggling girls promised to join them to cool off in the shade of the grape trees, they buried their textbooks and rolled up their shirtsleeves. When he found out his son was skipping classes for some experimental Biology, Neville's father begged me and Joel to talk to him.

We walked round one Sunday, sat Neville down and gave him chapter and verse. After the tongue-lashing he got back to his studies. Top in History, second in Science, me and Joel bought him a new satchel when he showed us his next report. Imagine our surprise then, when, a month later, we got a call from the principal for a meeting after school.

Levi Neptune was thirty, and yes, young for a principal. One look at his Canadian certificates, and the Ministry promoted him to bring some discipline and sanity to the school. At least that was the talk in the district.

But he looked as strong as the trunk of a guava tree. Powerful shoulders and a thick neck backed this up ten times over. The broad face looked kind, tipping him on the plus side of handsome. As I was running my eyes over the office, I was sure he was sizing up me and Joel in return. He kept glancing at the window, he was like a man carrying a basket-load of worries trying to make out he was on the way to a spree. What was he struggling to put out of his mind?

'Sorry about the short notice,' he began. 'I called Neville's father, but he said he passed him over to the two of you.'

'He used to be such a good pupil.' It was just like Joel to apologise in advance. 'He was always showing off his Chemistry, asking me questions I had to look up when I got home.'

'I know,' Mr Neptune said, his smile backing up his words. 'If you ask some students to tidy the classroom they stretch out their left hand for a ten-dollar bill, and the right hand for five as a bonus. But not Neville. He does it because he's that kind of boy.'

'So what happened this time?' Joel wanted to know.

'The old problem is back. Neville can't shift bad company. He and two girls crept into the IT room and changed the settings for the school computers.'

Joel made a braying noise like a final warning from a donkey to an irritating fly.

'They what?'

'Knocked out the monitoring system. For three hours yesterday, the pupils could visit *any* website – and you know what some youngsters are like.'

'The system is fixed now?' Joel asked.

'Yes.' Mr Neptune sounded relieved. 'Good thing we took on two IT specialists this year. They were there till seven working on it.'

'What did you do to the culprits, suspend them?'

The headmaster handed Joel a copy of the letter he had given the pupils to take home.

'Final warning.'

'I'll talk to him again,' my husband promised. 'He's a good boy at heart, let me see if I can drill some sense into him.'

We spent the next five minutes on a 'care plan' to help Neville catch up, then we left, a bit annoyed with him but hopeful.

My husband loves ital food, but every now and again he gets this craving for cake, and he would pester me till I give in and bake a couple. I was in the kitchen on the Saturday afternoon trying to put off gathering eggs and butter and flour and cinnamon and bowl and essence, when someone rapped on the front door. Thank you, visitor – I clasped my hands in prayer before my eyes – Cassie's just not in a baking mood today.

I opened the door and found the headmaster standing there. Hands in his pockets, he looked like a lover who couldn't wait for night to see his mistress, and was now regretting his rashness. He was sporting a purple T-shirt, black cords and brown sandals. Trendy dark glasses also, to round off the casual look. Off duty in every way. I let him in, expecting news that Neville was back in Rabacca picking grapes or fat pork with a girl.

'Good afternoon headmaster,' I said, 'don't often see you in these parts.'

'Call me Levi, please,' he begged. 'No school on Saturdays.'

'So then, Levi, social visit?'

He gave a half-smile, the lover getting cold feet. 'Yes and no,' he answered.

He followed me to the back of the house where me and Joel relaxed, and took the closest chair.

'Wonderful view of the Caribbean Sea,' he said.

'Thanks. Something to drink?'

'Some juice, please, too early for a *strong*.'

I fixed him a soursop topped with cinnamon, and sat facing him. He took a large swallow then said in a whisper, as if he was afraid the sea might hear us, 'Cassie: can I call you Cassie?'

'I'm fine with that.'

He cleared his throat then leaned forward. 'Mrs Providence, I need your help.'

'Help with what?'

He pulled out an A5 envelope from his right trouser pocket and passed it to me.

'Someone sent me this letter, and it's keeping me up at night. Here.'

I took the envelope and drew out the letter. It was typed on lilac printing paper, no date, no address.

Headmaster, I am deeply disturbed by the example you are setting your staff. You, the man who swore to clean up the school and set high standards. Yet what do you do? You prey on the young vulnerable female teachers! Poor women, imagine how they must feel day after day hearing you pontificating, when they know what your hands and lips get up to when no one is around. Desist, headmaster, or I will make your dirty deeds public!

Public Servant

When I came to the end I looked up at Mr Neptune.

'It's not true,' he said before I could ask who, why or what. 'Not a word or sentence.'

The letter had to be from someone with connections at the school. The flowery language? Well, some people go in for that kind of thing, I suppose.

'Any idea who sent it?' I asked.

'No.'

'You're sure?'

'Positive.'

There was no stamp on the envelope. 'How did you get the letter?' I asked.

'I found it in the porch one morning a while back. Big and bold, right on the chair where I usually sit and read.'

'The person dropped it off during the night?'

'Had to be.'

'And he or she hasn't been in touch since?'

'Not directly.'

'Then how?' I asked.

He pointed to the envelope in my lap. 'Take another look inside.'

I felt a bit foolish for not realising there was more inside the envelope, but it was just a folded photocopy of a note.

Miss Ryan, I am saddened to hear that such an excellent teacher is giving in to the desires of the Headmaster. Don't think of denying it, I have the evidence passed to me in confidence. Cavorting in the office: not a pretty sight! Leave $1500 in an envelope under the stone at Bad John Corner at 8 pm next Friday, or your father will get an eyeful of pictures no parent ever wishes to see.

Public Servant

I looked up at the headmaster again. 'Who is Miss Ryan?' I asked.

'One of the new computing technicians we took on. Fantastic interview.'

'The stuff about the pictures, is *that* true?'

The headmaster screwed up his face as if I was accusing

him of stealing exercise books from the school, and selling them at the market in Kingstown.

'No,' he said strongly. 'When Miss Ryan showed me the note I was lost for words.'

'So you two don't have a thing?'

'No.'

'In the past?'

He shook his head. 'I can't stop it, Cassie,' he said, 'but I don't encourage staffroom romance. Coconut water and beer don't mix very well, and it's the same with work and play. Geography and Sociology teachers not on speaking terms because one likes to romance on Sunday, and the other the middle of the week, can wreck more than a lesson. Pupils have long eyes and sharp ears.'

Teachers chasing one another over desks and scattering chairs; textbooks, files, pens, pencils and boxes of chalk flying everywhere: I smiled at this image in my mind of the staff at Elma Francois Secondary giving in to their hormones. When the smile went, it hit me that I didn't know much about Mr Neptune outside his work. In SVG you couldn't help running into teachers. At the supermarket bidding for a discount, or at a service or a funeral singing low or too high. You even met them trying to jump the queue at a bank. How come I had never glimpsed this one, or heard rumours about him speeding, gambling or arguing over land?

He resembled a family man. Quiet, church-going, I could picture him visiting Jasper Rock Tunnel and Owia Salt Pond, and testing his children when they got home. For why else did he look a little petrified? Wasn't it fear that his loved ones might discover his after-school activities?

'Could be a bit tricky if your wife finds out what's in the letters,' I said.

Mr Neptune grinned nervously, if I didn't know better, I would have looked for an invisible hand softly tickling him.

'I'm not married,' he explained.

'Children?' I asked, for he wouldn't be the first or the last.

He made a clucking noise now, like a chicken first to the shade on a hot day.

'None. I'm not a Christian or anything like that, just that it never happened.'

'Some people might call you eligible then.'

He broke out in a laugh. 'Miss Ryan is young, Cassie, what would she be doing with a man like me?'

'I wasn't just thinking of Miss Ryan. Most of the staff are female, show them a single man with ambition, and who knows what might stir?'

'Only five of them are not spoken for.'

'Five potential admirers then!'

'Five good secret-keepers too!'

I got back to the case. 'When and where did Miss Ryan give you the letter?'

'After school last Thursday.'

'How was she?'

'Upset, worried, frightened – take your pick.'

'And the money?'

'She asked for an advance from her salary to pay it. She didn't know what evidence the blackmailer had, but I could understand her wish to keep her parents out of it.'

'So you gave her the money?'

'Yes.'

'As an advance?'

Mr Neptune drummed fingertips to fingertips silently.

'No,' he said, 'I told her she could pay me back when she had the funds.'

'And *Public Servant* hasn't been in touch since?'

'No.'

'What's your worry, then?'

He stared at the sea for a while. 'My mind tells me there's more to come. And I don't wait the school mixed up in bohbohl. Academic results are up, lateness down, sports flourishing, the pupils are respectful. After all the work the staff and pupils have done to pull Elma Francois up, that would be a real shame.'

'And you want me to find out who he is?'

'Or she.'

'She?'

'Why not? Women make up half the world, they're just as devious and malicious as men.'

After this swinging delivery, Mr Neptune got up. I didn't push him for his suspicions, finding things out was *my* work. Sometimes it was best to begin with a clean slate.

My husband came home when Mr Neptune was probably three miles into his journey if he was a slow driver. I was making up a new case file when Joel pushed open the door carrying a bottle of port by the neck.

'Cake,' he mumbled. 'I can't smell baking, I can't smell cake.'

'Sorry honey.' I tried to butter him up with the butter I should have used in the kitchen. 'Sorry sweetheart, but something came up.'

'Something like what?'

'A case.'

Three frown lines creased his forehead. 'What case?'

I gave him the verse on the headmaster's visit, then threw in a sweet smile. He listened in a kind of way, then turned away to go and change. After his roast breadfruit and stewed saltfish dinner he went to the porch vex vex. The rest of the evening he sat there counting the green plums on the neighbour's tree. Just as well she didn't put on her music, or he would have gone over to switch it off himself. When I rubbed his forearm later that night all I got was a hunch of the shoulders.

It was the end of term a fortnight later, freedom for the teachers from their pupils, and from more paperwork from the Ministry of Education. To celebrate, the school had an outing to Canouan on the last day. The headmaster invited me and Joel along, and five other parents. We were 'special guests', but I didn't mind what he called us. If he wanted someone to take the sting of the teachers, why not? On the ferry over I did my best to mingle with the staff, no notebook, just an eye and an ear for letter writers and fancy talkers.

Up on deck some of the female teachers read magazines or dozed quietly. The men? A bunch of them stood at the side of the boat like explorers, pointing to the sea and arguing about tides and currents. I sat with the four Science teachers when the sea got choppy, hoping my old CXC basic pass grade wouldn't leave me exposed. The lab equipment was a disgrace, a woman whispered to me as if I had connections in high places, the Ministry was asking her to make satin bakes from flour alone.

Humanities was next, two men and seven talkative women. No moans, thankfully, but a short poetry session. Mervyn Tittle recited some Shake Keane verses, what could be better on a long sea journey? I eased away from the Maths team when they switched to discussing imaginary numbers, the computer technicians, Eutrice Ryan and Dexter Bluefield had to be softer company.

These two were sitting together on the port side of the ship. As I got close I heard them hissing and squawking. They sounded like a married couple arguing over who should sleep by the window. Don't interfere, Cassie girl, I told myself, catch them when they're in a better mood.

I walked past the pair to watch the fish racing the ferry, a school of eight having their daily treat. Did my father enjoy this sight too on the journey to and from Mayreau? When I returned to the technicians the bedroom row was over, but another one was simmering. About salaries and promotion this time, and the cost of travelling to work. The kitchen was getting hot too, it was best not to enter.

Once at the beach, the outing truly came alive. It might have been the sun or the warm sea, but I suspect that the drink and food played a part. Bottles of *Hairoun* and harder stuff popped out of heavy bags, fried fish and chicken, roast breadfruit and homemade bread spread themselves on towels like a minor miracle. The staff had clearly come to fete.

Imagine a family out for a picnic, with a few close friends tagging along to add some spice, and you had the gang of teachers and the school support team. Swimming, sharing food and drink, not a single miserable face was in sight. When the caretaker connected a speaker to his mobile, the staff of Elma Francois Secondary jigged away the cares of the old term like a bunch of teenagers at a disco with the lights off. And their guests too, of course.

After feeding and a long bathe – and too many beers – the headmaster nodded for the caretaker to restart the music.

'Ladies,' he.slurred and stretched each word. 'Dear ladies, time for a reel. For your dedication in a tough term, I'm going to take you all for a short spin. From senior to junior, and those in between.'

I nudged Joel who was cruising along Liquor Street himself. 'This could be fun,' I said to him. 'A groggy headmaster, a troupe of tipsy women, shouldn't we try to talk Neptune out of it?'

'Leave the man alone,' Joel replied, 'let the staff see his personal side.'

He wasn't wrong. Like ladies at a grand ball, the women were happy to join in the festive mood. Some dug up a pretty waltz from their girlhood, others wriggled legs and toes – not much waist – nothing to make their pupils or children cover their eyes in embarrassment. I looked on, getting ready to tap out a few steps in case the headmaster was too soaked to separate me from his female staff.

I wasn't the only one stewing. When Eutrice Ryan's turn was coming up, I saw her tiptoe away to an almond tree by the road. The next moment she was wrapping a towel around her like a girl under a chill. Joel touched me on the shoulder and pointed to Dexter drifting over to her. We watched argument number three, arms slicing the air, 'bad eye' for 'bad eye'. Miss Ryan didn't seem an easy woman to persuade.

'Migraine,' Dexter reported to a disappointed-looking Mr Neptune when he got back to the frolic. 'It's the heat. Even as a girl it affected her.'

'What a pity,' the headmaster said sadly. 'What a shame.'

Why would Eutrice Ryan embarrass the principal like that? Was she fretting about *Public Servant*, or was she afraid she might give away some secret as Mr Neptune grooved her?

At 4.30, home time, the cameras came out. The men took the headmaster's hand and posed, the women planted loud kisses on his cheeks when he could steady himself. Apart from Eutrice Ryan, the female teachers seemed fine with their young leader.

After the fun and games at the beach, the return journey dragged. Once the ferry began to bounce on the waves – typical Vincies – the passengers started to snooze. I was a little unsteady, but I had work to do. The teachers were dozing in little clusters, but guess who was sitting by herself gazing at the dusk closing in?

I went and sat beside Eutrice Ryan, on the starboard side.

She was wearing a plum-coloured, knee-length, button-down dress. Up close I saw that she was quite good-looking.

Her skin had a sumptuous black glow. She had large, liquid black eyes, a shapely nose, and full, luscious lips. If she added earrings and a silver necklace, she might have more than *Public Servant* watching her moves.

'How's the headache?' I asked, like a concerned sister.

She looked me over then replied, 'Better,' in a gruff voice.

'And the sunstroke?'

'The sun gone in,' she snapped. 'What happen, you blind?'

I sapped up the sharp reply. 'Enjoyed the day out?'

She shrugged now, and I was grateful for this scrap from her table. 'Better than work.'

'How's the job going?'

She gave me a nervous look that quickly turned to a nasty one. 'You from the Ministry or something?'

'Me?' I said the first thing that came into my mind. 'Na, I'm a guest of the principal.'

For some reason this made her soften. 'You're related to Mr Neptune?'

'Something like that.'

She was softer still. 'Truly?'

'Yes.'

'I didn't know that.'

'You know him well?'

'We talk – the principal is very approachable.'

'Why didn't you want to dance with him then?'

She stared at me as if I had pointed out the grains of sand by her left ear the towel had missed.

'Where did you get that from?' she scowled.

'When your turn was coming up you ducked out.'

I could see her struggling to come up with a reply.

'I'm not a good dancer.'

'You were flexing before.'

'Look.' She was back to the woman with a temper. 'Look,

are you my *keeper* or something? Do I have to explain what I do and don't, and why, to you?'

I held up a hand. 'Ease up young lady. You seemed a little sad. I was only trying to keep you company for a while.'

Miss Ryan got up, grabbed her bag, and showed me her pretty teeth.

'Thanks,' she growled, 'but I don't want company: yours or anybody else!'

In a rocking boat on a heaving sea, she crossed to the opposite side of the deck.

She was sitting filing her nails a while later when Dexter went and sat beside her. I saw them whispering, and two pairs of hands flapping like windscreen wipers in heavy rain. Before the rain could ease, she was pointing Dexter to the back of the ferry. Two-nil to Eutrice Ryan, if not three, I said to myself.

As the lights twinkled in Kingstown harbour, I noticed the sorrowful look she had. Did she receive another letter from *Public Servant*? Was she so in love with Mr Neptune that the other women made her jealous? What exactly was bugging her?

My scribbles later that night were hard to read the following day. The trip had given me a headache, but not much more. The headmaster was popular, the staff mixed easily. A few griped like babies with thrush, but all agreed he was trying his best. If he was involved with a teacher she was either Miss Extremely Discreet or Mrs Absent. *Public Servant's* claim that he was putting pressure on the female teachers didn't hold up. So where to next?

I went in search of the rumours that circulate in any workplace, and this meant to see the staff of Elma Francois, but this time one-on-one. At home, on their own, would they stick to their story from the trip, or would they let out what they truly felt in confidence?

I spent two days visiting them to 'thank' them for 'inviting' us on the day out. What made the school tick, I asked discreetly, which teachers brought in little gifts? I found most of them at home, reading, cooking, relaxing, or looking after their children. No matter what I asked they didn't fault their leader. Yes, he worked them hard – they said – but he worked himself even harder. Last on my list, Miss Ryan wasn't feeling well, her mother said, she was in bed with a fever.

Mrs Hudders from Adelphi was holidaying in Barbados with her sister, I found out on Day 2, Mr Clarke from Bridgetown took me to the fields where he was looking after his goats. According to two small boys playing marbles at Dexter Bluefield's gate, he was fixing his bike in Kingstown. 'Pistons', said the older boy, 'rings', the other added. If the staff were all on the same chorus or difficult to contact, that only left the pupils. What were they up to? Messaging with a vengeance on their phones? Playing cricket or fishing for lobsters? Netball? Bible Studies?

'I'm thinking of dropping by the park on Tuesday,' I told Joel on the third day. 'The netball team is practising for a match.'

'So?' he asked.

I knew I sounded feeble, but I didn't care.

'Children run a school,' I tried to sound casual, 'they see and hear more than the staff, they know the runnings inside out.'

Joel glared at me as if I was the police cadet who fainted when he asked her to draw a semiquaver.

'Cassie, you catch sunstroke or something?' he said. 'You going to act on children's talk?'

'What you call talk,' I answered, hoping he wouldn't call me desperate to my face, 'is what I call background intelligence.'

One evening at the park was my plan and, luckily, it did

the trick. I watched as the girls ran and pivoted and caught the ball in skirts so short, tight, and revealing, that an army of boys vied to coach them in a sport they would never play. And Neville was right in the middle. 'Jump higher,' you couldn't miss the deep rumbling voice, 'run slower so you could catch better.'

In the cool evening I sat behind two substitutes, Bertha Marriaqua and Petra Leclerc, who were waiting their turn to play. You can't get children to where you want them without a steer, so I took the two girls via the latest Skinny Fabulous song, the trouble I was having setting a new ringtone, to finding someone to fix my laptop. No points for guessing whose names came up. Petra voted for Miss Ryan, Bluefield was the man, according to her friend. I sat back and listened.

'Dexter really have it bad for Miss Ryan, you know,' Bertha tittered under the floodlights. 'But Eutrice like a mullet – she not biting.'

'She like him too,' Petra said, 'but he too boastful.'

'Boastful how?'

'He always acting like he is *Senior Technician*, brining in the latest computer packages, and trying to tell her how to do her job.'

'He's the boss, what's wrong with that?'

'Boss, my derriere. Believe me, Miss Ryan in charge.'

'No way. Dexter controlling things.'

I thanked the girls, wished them good luck in the game, and left.

I drove to Prospect to see Mr Neptune several days later. Students got their reports once a term, the head wasn't that patient. He showed me up the stairs into a house that was well kept but needed a woman's fussiness. He offered me a cup of mint tea, made himself a coffee, and we sat looking out at a grey Battowia.

'I feel like I'm walking backwards up a steep hill, Levi.' I always found it best to admit the truth. 'I've been following the staff and they're just enjoying their holidays. No one refused to talk to me, not a single screw face. Eutrice and Dexter are the only two I didn't see, what's going on with them? Both seem to think they're in charge of the computing section.'

'I don't know why,' the head replied, 'they're on the same grade, same pay. Equal in every way.'

'One is a good-looking young woman,' I pointed out.

'I've never done anything to encourage Eutrice. Ever since I took them on, I've tried my best to be fair.'

'What did they do before joining the school?'

'Eutrice worked at the Treasury in Kingstown, and Dexter was a librarian in Antigua: excellent references, both of them.'

'Why switch jobs, IT pays that much more?'

'About $8 000 a year, but it's not about the money. Eutrice is looking to train as an English teacher, and Dexter is hoping to become a computer programmer.'

'Unusual?'

'Perhaps. But pick any pupil in the schoolyard and ask anything about a PC, and just sit back and listen. Elma Francois is lucky to have Ryan and Bluefield.'

'They're that good?'

'Definitely.'

'If you had to pick, who would be number one?'

I could see the headmaster choosing his words carefully.

'Eutrice stands in if a teacher is absent, Dexter makes sure pupils can use the full range of software packages. Different skills, same high level.'

'A good combination,' I said.

'That's what I told them at their probation interview.'

'What did they say to that?'

160

'Well, Dexter was first, and he seemed pleased with my report. He gave me a hug and left.'

'And Eutrice?'

'She followed Dexter, and she seemed happy too. But it was a pity – she said – that the teachers earned so much more than the technicians.'

'She wanted more money?' I asked.

'She didn't put it like that.' The headmaster was quick to defend her, I noticed.

'Then how?'

'She wanted me to upgrade her, and to put in a good word at the Ministry.'

'And did you?'

'I would help in any way I could,' I told her, 'but the Ministry of Education has a mind of its own, as you know.'

When I left the principal's home that morning, I thought I might as well drive the Toyota round in circles, for that was how the case had me.

Mr Neptune's prediction came true the third week of the holidays. On the Wednesday he phoned and asked me to meet him at a snackette in Kingstown. Extremely important, he whispered, most urgent.

When I got there, it looked like the kind of place to take a friend you're trying to shake off. He bought two bottles of coconut water then, before I could raise my eyebrows about his choice of eating place, a photograph was sliding up from his briefcase. He passed it to me, shifting in his chair like a man about to ask forgiveness for the sins he might one day commit.

The picture showed him in his office, left hand by his side, and the other hand somewhere else. Eutrice Ryan's arms were locked tenderly about his neck. A puzzled look and a wide-eyed surprise were his only defence.

'Well?' I said, after a brief scan of the picture, trying my best not to sound like a Jehovah's Witness.

The headmaster made a nibbling sound like a hungry rabbit then said, 'Miss Ryan phoned me this morning, she got a copy too. It's a frame-up, you know, what's in the picture didn't happen.'

'You mean the two of you in a clinch?' I couldn't resist saying.

'It wasn't a clinch, I didn't make a move on her.'

'So she did the running, did she?' I asked.

'If you want to call it that, yes.'

'And you gave in.'

'We didn't kiss or anything like that.'

'Didn't you?'

'No.'

'Why not?'

'I told Eutrice that if she was serious about me, we would have to talk about it. But not there. And not then.'

'And when you *did* talk about the two of you?'

Mr Neptune cleared his throat, and his gaze shied away from me. 'We haven't.'

'Why not?'

'Miss Ryan is shy, Cassie. And – how can I put it – I don't have a lot of experience with women.'

Two shy people hugging up and kissing at lunchtime, lucky thing it wasn't after school.

'When was the picture taken?' I asked.

'Just after she passed her probation.'

'Who was the photographer?'

'I don't know, no one else was in the office.'

'It was just the two of you?'

'Yes.'

'Headmaster, you need to come clean and tell me exactly what happened that day.'

Mr Neptune put down the bottle of coconut water and leaned forward to explain.

'I emailed the technicians that morning to come and see me, Bluefield first, then Miss Ryan. Bluefield came at 12.15, I congratulated him, and told him to keep up the good work. Not long after Miss Ryan was there. Same speech – I try to be fair. The next thing I knew she was wrapping her arms round my neck and whispering that she had feelings for me.'

'And who just happened to pass by the window when she was kissing you? One of the students? A member of staff? The security officer? A parent?'

'Could be anyone, Mrs Providence, my door is always open.'

'Anything unusual about the picture?' I asked. 'Any clues to the sender?'

'No.'

'Did you study it closely?'

The principal closed his eyes. 'I can't bear to look at it, I'm so ashamed.'

I thought back to the evening in his office discussing Neville. A window was open to the left of his chair, this was probably the one through which the picture was snapped. From ground level I assumed, from one of the houses nearby, or from the shop across the road.

The office was like Mr Neptune's home, tidy, but a place to work. A large wooden desk, a computer, metal cabinets, a bookshelf, no family pictures to give it that personal touch. That evening his secretary had promised to bring in some flowers to brighten the place, and a watch to remind him to leave at six.

'Did your secretary ever buy you that watch for your birthday?' I asked now.

Mr Neptune took a drink of coconut water. 'No,' he said, 'I'm still waiting on Ameela.'

After the meeting I walked to the centre of town, to the police base where I was once a regular. Dominoes, draughts and cards were going on as usual. During a game of Black Jack with Peter Lowpillow, I listened in to the latest police news – van drivers speeding through towns and narrowly missing children, drug yachts, the usual bewildering stuff. Later, on the way to my car in Frenches, I glimpsed Eutrice Ryan leaving a bank. She was hugging a large briefcase and scurrying for the centre of town like someone late for an appointment. Track her or find out what was in the briefcase? My mind told me to check on her business at the bank.

Otis Quashie, one of the senior cashiers, was an old primary school friend who used to help me with my Geography. Every PI needs a little crew of helpers, and he was one of my best. I jumped the queue, went straight to Otis, asked about his father, and minutes later we were in an air-conditioned back office. On Mon 2nd, Wednesday 11th, Tuesday 17th, Eutrice Ryan withdrew $1000 from her account. Ninety dollars and a few cents were left, barely enough for a decent skirt. I thanked Otis, then went scouring the capital for the mysterious woman.

But there was no sign of the computer technician. Was she keeping an appointment, or was she enjoying a hearty lunch in some expensive restaurant?

I phoned Joel, it was time to drag out the old mix and mingle. Check out the bar Dexter Bluefield sometimes went to, I told him, keep an eye on the computer king. But there was no dirt to dig. No big spending, no standing everyone drinks. A quiet ginger beer over a game of draughts, that was Mr Bluefield. What me and my husband couldn't miss later that night, though, was Dexter parking his Yamaha motorbike in Miss Ryan's yard at nine, and pushing open the front door without rapping first. What the hell was going on?

By now the case was digging into me like the naked bedsprings in a tired mattress. Weeks prying into the affairs of the staff, and where was I? One day feeling positive, the next like a dunce in Infant School. My body tense at night, it was difficult to switch on to being a wife.

What was it about the case that humbugged me so much? It seemed so simple, that was probably the reason. The two main suspects took me so far then left me high and dry. When we got home that night I got out my notebook and studied the entries one more time.

Eutrice Ryan stayed indoors most days – my notes showed – some evenings she went for a long stroll at dusk, alone, no girlfriend or boyfriend to enjoy the sights with. Her trips to Kingstown shopping ended with lunch at Bev's Restaurant with a large plate of rice and a cold lime juice for company. Dexter Bluefield disappeared for hours each day on his motorbike, he rode so fast my car couldn't keep up with him. He sometimes played cards in a bar in Sion Hill, twice in one week I spotted him giving Eutrice a ride home on his bike after her evening walk.

Two letters and a photo that gave the principal sleepless nights, why didn't the blackmailer ask for money this time? Miss Ryan was happy to ride on Dexter's bike, was Bluefield her true lover? Were they forever falling out and making up? Was Miss Ryan teasing the headmaster while carrying on with her computing colleague?

I woke up in a temper early one morning and went for a drive. Joel knew the kind of woman I was, he would understand my need to go it alone, or to find a quiet place to sit and reflect.

I drove for seven miles then parked close to the beach near the Ryan home. I sat on a rock staring at the Caribbean Sea for inspiration. Was the female giant on her way up from Grenada? If so, where would she be now, on Palm Island?

I was wondering this, and taking in the brilliant morning colours when bam! who did I spot strolling along the beach tossing pebbles at the sea and racing each other? Eutrice and Dexter, the couple who were supposed to be at war! And to round off the dawn frolic, why wasn't I surprised when, an hour later, they disappeared into the house where Eutrice lived with her parents?

When I got home I told Joel about the early birds at the beach. My husband looked grey and sickly, like a man on a low-protein diet, and small portions at that.

'Secret lovers?' he asked, rubbing the sleep from his eyes.

'Not so secret,' I replied. 'They stepped into the house in broad daylight!'

'You mean Miss Ryan is pretending she loves the headmaster, but running around with Bluefield?'

'Seems like it.'

'Only one thing to do then,' Joel suggested.

'What's that?'

'Confront her. Ask her to explain.'

I knew Joel was right, but how was I going to engineer a meeting with Eutrice? I couldn't simply waltz up to her house and ask her to swap recipes for cake. She had no idea I was watching her, and I didn't want her parents or neighbours involved. What to do?

Fetching my magnifying glass, I examined the picture the headmaster got in the post, going over every square inch this time. I went over Eutrice's dress and hair, I studied the layout of the room. And then all of sudden, bam! again, things became clear. I ran the magnifying glass over the photo until there could be no doubt. Yes, the picture was clear now!

I phoned Mr Neptune and asked him to get Eutrice Ryan to the school. He could use his authority, he could lay on the charm, he could invite her in for a personal holiday detention. All I wanted was for her to be there at eleven.

Miss Ryan was prompt. She had combed out her hair and clipped it with a pony comb at the back. Her yellow shift dress grazed her knees, it was a bit plain-Jane, but the perfume she had sprayed on made up for the country-girl look. When she saw me she screwed up her face.

'What you doing here?' she grumbled, as I entered the computer room.

'Interview,' I said quickly. 'For the new governor. Just taking a look round the building.'

She looked at me suspiciously. 'I thought you said you're related to the headmaster.'

'We're second cousins.'

'So why he's interviewing you?'

'To make sure I can do the job properly.'

'The principal is something else, isn't he?'

'In what way?' I asked.

'This is SVG,' she explained, 'relatives don't have to suffer interviews, the job is automatic.'

'So well done, Mr Neptune?'

'Definitely. I really admire the principal.'

'*Admire*, or more than that?'

'What's above *admire*?'

I helped her out. 'Love?'

She answered with a nervous laugh then fell silent.

'Do you love him?' I asked when the silence stretched too long.

Eutrice Ryan walked to the window and stared at the field of sweet potatoes to the north of the school.

'Yes, I do love him, Mrs Providence,' she said with her back to me. 'It's terrible, isn't it?'

'Why is it terrible?'

She turned and came and stood next to me.

'Because I love the headmaster, but the love has to be one-way. Levi doesn't allow relationships in school. You can't make a rule then break it, can you? If he showed feelings for me, he would end up in a trap like a manicou.'

'And if things were different?'

Miss Ryan covered her eyes with her left hand as if confessing love is a weakness. 'I would tell him what is in my heart, and ask if it was the same for him.'

I waited for this to sink in then said, 'He told me about the letter. And I have the photo of the two of you in the office.'

She gave a brave, sickly smile like a girl wrestling with her first bra, but refusing help.

'I was so ashamed and frightened when I got it,' she said, 'I locked the picture in my suitcase.'

'Any idea who *Public Servant* is?' I asked.

She bit into her bottom lip. 'No.'

'You're an attractive young woman, you must have a good heap of admirers.'

'The principal is the only man I care for.'

'But some other man might care for you.'

'That is his concern.'

'And *Public Servant*?'

'*Public Servant* is a coward, Mrs Providence. He took money I can't afford, he is blackmailing me and threatening the principal. *Public Servant* is no better than the stone where you hang out your panty to dry.'

I smiled to myself. 'What will you do if he sends more pictures and asks for more money?'

'No more pictures to send. That was the only time me and Levi got close.'

Was she telling the truth, or was she playing a role to perfection? I watched her carefully, studied the eyes, took in the face. Did she truly love the principal, or was it all an elaborate set up? As I was wondering this, the door opened and Mr Neptune entered.

'Lunch, ladies,' he whispered in the happy sing-song voice of a man who has paid all his monthly bills and has enough left over to throw a party. 'My office.'

I made to follow him, but Eutrice Ryan hesitated.

'You too, Miss Ryan,' Mr Neptune said with a verve I didn't know he had in him. 'Come nuh, woman.'

There were three paper plates on the headmaster's desk, all with fat inviting rotis.

'One beef, one fish, one chicken,' Mr Neptune sounded so sparky I was afraid his blue shirt and brown trousers might catch fire. 'Pick your favourite, ladies. And I'll take the fish roti that's left.'

We both raised a smile, and Eutrice Ryan held out a hand for me to have first go. I selected the beef, and she lifted the chicken.

Mr Neptune took his roti and hefted it. 'Thank you, ladies.'

I ate slowly, trying to line up the picture sitting in my bag with the actual layout of the office. Yes, things were clear now. The photo was the key. I was sipping a grapefruit juice when there was a knock on the door.

Mr Neptune looked quizzically at me and Miss Ryan.

'Funny,' he said, 'I didn't tell anyone I was at the school today. Did either of you?'

'No,' me and Eutrice Ryan answered together.

He got up, opened the door, and in stepped Dexter Bluefield in his motorbike gear.

'I was in the area,' he said brightly, 'thought I would drop in to carry out a quick scan of the computers for viruses, and update some software.'

The headmaster waved him in. 'That's good of you Dexter, man, pull up a chair.'

The moment Dexter joined us Miss Ryan's face changed.

She looked tense, pressing down on her chair as if praying for the floor to let her through.

'Just finished lunch, Bluefield,' Mr Neptune said, 'if I knew you were coming by, I would have got you a roti too.'

Dexter smiled to tell him he was fine. 'I took a bite at Fernandez down the road.'

'Next time then,' said Mr Neptune, like two fellas with a rum shop in common.

'Hold you to that.'

After the rum talk it was my turn. Four people crammed into a small hot room, it was time to get at the case.

'I'm glad you're here, Dexter,' I began. 'I want your help with something.'

'Consider it fixed,' he said. 'And if it's software, I can do you a good price.'

'It's not my computer,' I explained.

'What then?'

'I need your help with a couple of questions.'

'Me? Questions?' he answered, sounding as cool as he looked in his riding gear.

'Yes,' I said.

'What about?'

'Oh nothing much,' I said casually. 'Just two letters and a photo.'

'What letters and photo?'

I tossed up a medium-pacer half-volley, no swing, straight as an arrow.

'Do you always do your duty, Mr Bluefield?' I said.

'What are you talking about?'

'Your duty as a public servant.'

'You're conversing in riddles, Mrs Providence.'

It was time to up the pace like the West Indian bowlers of old.

'Teachers, technicians, civil servants, farmers, the ordinary women and men of SVG: if they spot something wrong, they head to the police station, don't they?'

Bluefield didn't have to think about it. 'Naturally.'

'So if you saw something in the school you didn't like, you would do your duty, won't you?'

'Yes, I suppose I would.'

'What about blackmail?' I said casually, as if we were at a meeting to decide how many boxes of blue chalk to order.

Dexter was on his feet like a spectator about to celebrate three straight fours at the Arnos Vale Cricket Ground.

'Blackmail,' he hollered, 'what brand of nonsense you alluding to?'

'Sit down, Mr Bluefield,' I said softly. 'Please. Sit down.'

He remained standing. When he realised I wasn't going to make a fuss he went back to the chair.

'How about a lesson, Dexter,' I said when he was comfortable. 'You okay with that?'

'If it's short, yes.'

'Good,' I said, 'thank you. Now you signed up with the school to improve your computer programming, Miss Ryan wanted to train as a teacher. *You* were the IT champion, any class they gave Eutrice she was fine with. She was popular, and you got jealous. So at your probation interview an idea came into your mind and you thought, why not? You told Eutrice what happened at your meeting and threw in a little suggestion, hoping she would take the bait and give you a nice picture.'

Eutrice Ryan cut in then.

'Dexter said he gave the headmaster a hug to thank him. When I asked what I should do, he said a woman would give him a little peck on the cheek. That's what I did, but my feelings took over.'

171

'You knew the time of the meeting,' I continued, 'so you were waiting outside the window for the moment Eutrice was "thanking" Mr Neptune.'

Dexter Bluefield laughed. 'You have a wonderful imagination, Mrs Providence, you should switch to politics.'

'Only if you would be my treasurer,' I replied.

'No thanks. Computing is my love.'

'And money.'

'What money?'

'The programme is over, Bluefield, time to come clean.'

'I don't know what you're talking about.'

'But you do,' I said. 'Every week for the last month Miss Ryan has been emptying her account and leaving money in a secret spot. And guess who was gathering up the fat envelope?'

Mr Neptune looked confused and left out. He said, 'Eutrice, you didn't tell me you had fresh letters.'

Miss Ryan bowed her head. 'I didn't want to worry you,' she answered. 'I thought if I paid the blackmailer off, he would stop.'

'But he didn't stop,' I explained. 'The picture was going to be the start of another round: money from *both* of you this time. But, being an IT wizard, Dexter couldn't just send the *actual* picture of the two of you! He had to add a touch here, and another touch there.'

I took out three copies of the picture from my bag and passed them round.

'Look closely,' I said. 'In the picture you can see a clock on the wall behind the principal. Any clocks in this office? No. Mr Neptune doesn't use one. He took the picture at lunchtime, but take a look at the clock he dragged in. See it? What time is it showing? 7:15. You want more? Cast your eyes over the new Eutrice Ryan with neat diamond studs: Dexter couldn't help himself. Do you like the ring and the watch you're wearing, headmaster?'

Dexter Bluefield slipped off his riding gloves.

'It's all speculation,' he said, like a man who would deny his reflection in a mirror.

'Let the police decide,' I said. 'The picture, the letters written in your fancy librarian style, you're the one, Dexter.'

Mr Neptune had heard enough, he rushed to his feet.

'Bluefield, I'm ashamed of you,' he said. 'I took you on in good faith and you let me, and yourself down. And think of the hurt and pain you caused Miss Ryan.'

Bluefield shrugged. 'You don't have any proof. It could have been anyone of the staff.'

'No it's definitely you,' I said. 'And that's not even the cruel, heartless part. Twice you followed Eutrice when she went to place the money in the spot in your letter. And on her walk home, guess who turned up and offered her a ride? Fancy doing that to your sister!'

'Sister?' Mr Neptune turned to Eutrice with a look of total confusion. 'You're brother and sister?'

'Yes sir,' she bleated. 'Me and Dexter have the same mother but different fathers. He stole three registered letters from the post office so mom sent him to meet his father in Antigua.'

'Oh,' Mr Neptune said as if he didn't truly understand, and I could see him studying the two faces and trying to match the features.

'I told Dexter I was coming here today,' Eutrice explained, 'I didn't expect him to follow me.'

For an instant there was silence, and I could feel a blast of warm air. Then suddenly Dexter screamed out at Eutrice, then punched the nearest wall hard like you sometimes see in foreign films.

'You stupid girl, why don't you keep your mouth shut?'

Mr Neptune wasn't having that kind of behaviour in his office. He put Dexter in a headlock and squeezed him hard.

'Apologise!' he ordered him. 'Apologise to Eutrice!'

'Ekkke, Ekkke,' Dexter squeaked as Mr Neptune tightened his grip. 'Ekkkke.'

'Apologise!' the headmaster insisted. 'Say you're sorry!'

'Sorrekkke,' Dexter whimpered. 'Sorrekky.'

The principal released him then said calmly, as if he was sending Dexter on an errand to pick up some stationery. 'Mr Bluefield, take yourself out of my office. Get out now before I have to kick you out like a dog! And you make sure you return the money tomorrow. All of it, plus thirty per cent interest! Write a programme to calculate the amount if you can't work it out!'

Dexter Bluefield collected his riding gear, gave us each a bitter look, then shuffled away. When I heard him cranking his motorbike I got up. Mr Neptune had taken Eutrice Ryan's hand, a woman has to know when to make herself scarce.

'Thanks Mrs Providence,' Eutrice said as I was getting my bag. 'Thank you.'

'No problem,' I answered. 'Good luck.'

'We'll talk later Cassie,' Mr Neptune nodded. 'I'll drop by this evening.'

I shook my head so he would get the message. 'Any night but tonight.'

The moment Joel walked in after five I knew we were in for a late night. I had baked three cakes, they had come out like my aunt Jestina used to make them. The gorgeous aroma took over upstairs as well as down. Next time – I promised myself – I would bake without waiting for my husband to ask.

As usual, when I closed a case, Joel got excited.

'What did Miss Ryan have to say? Did she and Dexter confess?'

'Tell you about it tomorrow.'

'But what happened?'

'Cake, Joel,' I said. 'You can't smell cake?'

The port was out of the fridge before I could spell the word *ice*.

Joel took out two of our best glasses, and I followed him with the cake.

cassie and the sad wife

At Police College the instructors closed every session with a simple caution.

'Recruits,' each one reminded us, as if our heads were logs of cedar wood, 'don't take sides in a dispute, know and keep the proper distance.'

Before we could scatter for a cold mauby or tamarind juice, Sergeant Stoute would step forward, tall and bursting with fitness. That rich moustache without a strand of grey, no officer was more commanding. He would use his softest voice on us.

'Malicious neighbours spreading rumours; rich uncles or elderly tanties re-calling a birthday present; school friends jealous of your A grade; self-important lawyers who arrange an appointment at eleven and keep you waiting till two; the butcher who sells family and friends first, then fills your bowl with bones for the same price: treat them all with respect. Stay professional, don't bring your feelings into it.'

What was coming next was no surprise, but no Vincy throat or rib could resist the tickle.

'Girlfriend chasing boyfriend with a hoe,' the sergeant would invite us to imagine the scenario. 'What to do?'

Staff lowered, some trainee would mimic Stoute. 'Persuade her to use the hoe to dig arrowroot, sergeant?'

'Or yams. Don't swap places with the girl, don't imagine you are that country-boy either. Never wonder what you would do in their place. Invite them to talk it out in the privacy of home. No sides, no favours.'

Easy to say, not so easy to obey in a small country like SVG, where connections, looks, and tender kisses speak louder than talent or hard work. My trials took longer than most so, like a lover on a mission, I was well prepared.

Test one came months into my service. I was first on the scene when a jeep tore the bumper off a Volvo in a supermarket car park. A clear case of wrong and stupid. The jeep belonged to Nanton Watson from Tourama, who once made a footstool for my father. A nervy little man in thick glasses, he took me to one side and rubbed my forearm gently, as if what he did with his wife at night might work with me.

He pointed to the shining metal on the floor. 'Just a little dent, Cassie. Give me a "squeeze", eh? Back have to scratch back, not true?'

I didn't answer yes, I didn't say no. Instead I turned him round. 'Sorry,' I told him, 'bargain with the owner. See the lady coming.'

Not long after, on a Friday when I was off duty, Travise Davis, a fifteen-year old pupil from Union Island, rammed into my side as I was eyeing up a large roasting breadfruit at the market. Huffing and puffing some way behind was a shopkeeper hollering 'Damn Thief' at the top of her voice. Travise was a pretty girl with a short boyish haircut in school uniform of white and red. Her stomach was rising and falling so fast under her white blouse I thought she might faint.

'Thank goodness is you, Cassie,' she said. 'Look in my purse and count dollars. Do I look like a common thief? Your grandmother and my grandfather were first cousins on the Mulraine side of the family, you know!'

This was a surprise to me, but baking under the sun in Kingstown market wasn't the place to discuss our family tree.

'Really?' I said.

Travise made the sign of the cross. 'Cross my heart,' she said, 'but I have a ferry to catch. Deal with my terror for me.'

I took my latest cousin by the shoulder and gave her a little squeeze. 'New police code, Travise, every girl for herself now.'

'You'll make me miss my ferry!'

'Sorry, cousin.'

The next time I saw her she told me she was hoping to go to Community College. I bought her lunch, that Friday's slate was now clean. In the case of a young wife, I remembered Nanton and Travise, but almost forgot my training.

I was walking home a neighbour's seven-year-old daughter from a clinic one Monday afternoon when my phone went. The caller had a soft, careful voice.

'My name is Tammy Baptiste. Could you drop by *Baptiste Health Mixtures* on Middle Street?'

'I'm just on my way home, Miss,' I could hear myself mumbling, 'it's heated, my skin is itching, I need to shower and change.'

'I need your help, Mrs Providence,' Mrs Baptiste pleaded. 'Please?'

I didn't bother to change when I got in after I dropped off my charge. I picked up my notebook, and put my faith in the old vehicle.

Baptiste Health Mixtures was new to me. But then I wasn't one of the young Kingstown civil servants constantly seeking new places to eat and drink. The Baptiste family scoured the mainland and the Grenadines for fresh fruits and herbs, and blended them to order. Mangoes, plumose, guavas, sapodillas, mint, thyme, tamarind, no traveller to Kingstown did the trip without dropping in to sample a blend. Well, not according to

Mrs Baptiste, a short, solid woman with a wide flat face like a bammie, who opened the door to let me in.

'Thanks for coming at such short notice, Mrs Providence.'

'No problem,' I said, taking the stool she pointed me to.

She left me and went to the back of the shop. As I was flicking through their brochure, she returned with two large glasses with green straws poking out. She offered me the taller one and took a stool herself.

'Try this,' she said. 'Tamarind and turpentine mango with a sprinkling of cinnamon.'

I sucked in the drink and almost emptied the glass like a lickerish child. Mrs Baptiste sipped hers and watched me searching for the word to describe the heavenly mixture.

'It's my husband's favourite.'

'Tell him he has good taste,' I said. 'Now, what can I do for you?'

'It's our daughter.'

'What's the problem?'

'It's delicate, and I need help before all hell breaks loose and the police cart my husband to the jailhouse.'

I got the feeling this was going to be a tricky case, so I called Joel to explain that I might be late. Then I got out my notebook, sat back and listened.

'Our daughter, Barbara Verity, is thirty,' Mrs Baptiste began. 'Verity is her married name. She's five-three, fine features like her father. Such a lovely girl, Mrs Providence, and a good heart to go with it. She went to Barrouallie Secondary School then Community College, she studied hard and got A levels in Biology, Economics and Art. Good grades, me and my husband left school early, we were so proud of her. She was planning to work for a couple of years, save up, then apply to do a degree at UWI. But she fell pregnant at twenty-one, these things happen, don't they?'

I nodded and let her continue.

'We begged Barbara to wait, but she was desperate to get married before she began to show – in this day and age, I ask you.'

I wrote slowly, taking in the background, and trying to form a picture of Barbara.

'Her husband, Leroy, is a van driver. He's forty, and "popular" from Mount Wynne to Kingstown. He's up at five every morning to do the leeward to Kingstown passenger run. Some days he takes on up to twenty trips. On a quiet Wednesday he can bank well over five hundred dollars.

'For the first two years of marriage they seemed to get on well. Smart TV, English washing machine and dishwasher, huge American fridge, expensive laptops, the latest hi-fi system, Leroy didn't hold back, I'll grant him that. We can't afford half the luxuries they have. Early on someone pinched me about other women, but Barbara just laughed me away when I passed on the suspicion. Leroy was up at dawn, he had set her up in a lovely house overlooking the harbour, how many husbands did that for their family?

'Barbara works part-time in the business. She leaves at two on weekdays so she can collect their son Eli from school and fix dinner. But our once confident girl is now nervous and jumpy. The flesh is dropping off her. I'm sure she's catching hell with Leroy, and if she's not careful, she'll walk herself right into the mental home. And as long as I have the strength in me, I will make sure that doesn't happen.'

I put away the notebook, for I had a good idea now where we were going.

'First the change in her looks, second, the behaviour only someone long in the hills or overseas would miss. Barbara drives round every Saturday to do the accounts, but we didn't see her for three days. She didn't come to work, she wouldn't answer the phone, we found out she got a neighbour to pick up Eli from school.

'Then this morning she turned up wearing dark glasses. No explanation, no sorry, not a syllable. And she looked rough. Have you ever seen a Vincy woman with no faith in her figure and her pretty frocks? Her right eye had this puffy look, she is either bashing rum or she's covering up a blow. I phoned my husband to tell him she was back, he was so irate I had to plead with him not to come into town to deal with Leroy. He used to be a boxer, and he still trains three hours a day. If he gets his hands on the scamp, the police would have to scrape Leroy off the pavement to get him into the ambulance.'

'And what does Barbara say about the relationship?'

'I can't get much out of her these days. We used to talk and laugh like sisters, but I can't remember the last time I saw her smile. Do you know how heart-breaking that is, Mrs Providence? Which mother can stand by and watch their daughter fade into a shadow? Before she left I told her how worried I was, and asked her to trust me. She knows I struggle to do the books on my own, who or what prevented her calling?

'I'm sure she had tears in her eyes, but Barbara sat there and told me to my face that everything was fine at home. The swelling under her right eye? She and Eli were chasing a butterfly downstairs and she tripped. Why did she look so bagga-shagga, how come her clothes were hanging so loose? She was trying to drop off a stone in weight!

'I had to go to the storeroom and have a little cry, Mrs Providence.' Mrs Baptiste looked and sounded like she might cry now. 'The business is running nicely, but I feel such a failure.'

My mind went back to my police service as she took a rest and dabbed her eyes. To the tricky cases, and to the terrifying ones. This was going to be as tough as disarming a man who has lost everything, and who couldn't care who escorts him to hell, or how many.

'What exactly are you asking me to do?' I asked.

Mrs Baptiste gave me a pleading look. 'I want you to find out what Leroy is doing to Barbara.'

'Beware of a man-and-woman affair,' Sergeant Stoute used to plead, and his warning rang out in my head as we discussed fees and expenses and Mrs Baptiste counted out a deposit. 'Get the left-hand side of the story. A man can't fight himself; and the woman who tells you she doesn't get the urge to collar up her man every now and again for no good reason is a damn blasted liar!'

'Suppose Barbara is telling the truth?' I said to Mrs Baptiste. 'Suppose she and Leroy are just going through a rough patch? Marriages do, as you well know.'

Mrs Baptiste managed to raise a tiny smile.

'I realise that, Mrs Providence,' she replied. 'But I know our daughter, and you can't imagine how it hurts my heart to see her falling away like this. Such a clever girl, she could have been a UWI graduate, and what is she now? A woman afraid of her mirror, dragged down by a man who tramples all over her. Scared to read a book in her own home because Leroy is always snapping his fingers for her to fetch this and do that like a maid.'

Mrs Baptiste dried her eyes with the hem of her sleeve, then she got up.

'Gather the evidence and return our daughter to us, Cassie,' she begged. 'Too many years of her young life have gone on that good-for-nothing van driver. Time for her to dedicate some time to herself and her son.'

'Suppose she loves her husband despite everything?'

Mrs Baptiste glared at me, and I felt ashamed of myself for putting the question.

'You're a married woman, Cassie, you must know you can't truly love a man who has you in fear.'

Every case is tough, I reminded myself on the way to the car that Monday evening, if not sapping, then tricky. Getting between Barbara and her husband would be key. I would have to plan carefully for the task Mrs Baptiste just signed me up for, and take any luck going.

When I got home, I told Joel about the meeting. He could spot that I was tense and edgy, so he took my hand and guided me to my hammock. As he listened, he massaged my shoulders gently, ever so gently. In two-twos I was asleep.

'What to do, Joel?' I asked when we were in bed that night. 'How to begin a case like this?'

'Zzzzzzzzzzzz.'

I wasn't the only one feeling the strain at work.

'Check Leroy first,' he suggested when I made him fried plantains and strong black coffee next morning. 'See if he fills out the man Mrs Baptiste painted.'

'And if he doesn't?'

'Then return the deposit,' Joel came right back. 'You only have a case if you find out he's been roughing up Barbara.'

Joel's suggestion increased the feeling that this job was going to bruise a few people. Adding me to the total would make at least five of us.

Two days later, on the Wednesday, my husband drove me to Questelles at eleven. This was to be my first sighting of Leroy, and I had to keep sipping from a bottle of water my lips were so dry and coarse. Why I was so edgy I couldn't understand. Leroy didn't know me, yet my stomach kept churning over. At the back of mind, for some unknown reason, was the memory of the first time I came face to face with a drunkard in Jennings Valley swishing a cutlass at anyone and anything in his way.

As I sat in the car I was pensive and quiet, and Joel knew

it was best to let me alone when I was like that. We waited for Leroy's van to mount the hill from Clare Valley, then I got out the car. From the side of the road I watched Joel drive slowly away to drill his new batch of recruits. I felt like crying, I don't know why. It was as if he was leaving me for another woman.

At some stage I knew I would have to meet Leroy face to face, but I didn't want him to know I was *WARB*-ing him. I had bought a wig, some outsize glasses, and a print dress a cool fit for my grandmother. A black handbag too, stuffed with a change of clothes, binoculars, camera, scissors, notebook, and other tools of the trade. So the conductor guided a slow old woman with a large handbag to a tight space in the middle of a van crammed with passengers. Before my bottom could introduce itself properly to the seat, the vehicle was pulling away with hot tyres.

On most Caribbean islands a van licensed for twelve drives quietly from village A to town B, no rush, no flash, and there is order. Not in SVG. Drivers dress in fancy leather gloves and designer shades as though they are fighter pilots, or in felt hats, passengers put up with this posturing, but that isn't the worst part of it!

Most vans in SVG have a name, Leroy's van was called *Valentine*. It was a blue vehicle with comfortable seats and large windows. But the music! DDDmmm! DDDm! DDDmmmm! It was worse than the nastiest disco. The music thumped so hard I could almost feel it shaking the flesh off my bones. BDm! BDm! BDm! After five minutes of this pounding, I leaned forward and tapped the conductor on the shoulder.

'Tell the driver to turn it down a touch.'

The conductor was gangly, with short red hair to match his brown shirt and green shorts, as if it was permanently carnival season. A modern boy.

'An old lady here say the music too loud,' he passed on my request as he handed a fare to the driver.

At the next stop Leroy adjusted his brown felt hat, turned the dial to the left, and the granny got her answer.

'Tell she it have a next van right behind if the music not to her taste.'

A second later he pressed on the gas, *Valentine* shot off like a horse on a gallop, and my bottom said goodbye to the seat. I was still dangling in the air when the music flooded back to full volume. BBDDmm! BBDDmm! BBDDmm!

I tugged the conductor's forearm. 'Stop the damn vehicle. Let me off.'

In a stink of smoke and oil, not to mention noise, *Valentine* raced to a stop and I stumbled out. The conductor stretched a hand for the fare. I gave him a 'bad eye', pushed his hand away, and climbed out of *Valentine*. Minutes later I hailed the van behind. This one was quiet, I could enjoy the scenery, I could talk to my neighbour.

Back in Kingstown, after a fish roti and a cold mauby to steady myself, my plan was to hang around the Little Tokyo van terminal to try to gather some material on Leroy from the other drivers and passengers to Near Leeward. But on the way there, it came to me that I was overplaying my short ride an hour earlier. Ninety-six van drivers out of a hundred might have pushed their vehicle like Leroy. Short hop or long, they were hustlers competing for passengers, weren't they? Wasn't it survival of the fastest?

And of the loudest too. For, didn't some passengers choose a van for the thumping rhythms? Wasn't Leroy simply doing his best to earn a living for his family?

As usual the terminal was hot, noisy, pure chaos, like a beehive where the bees don't get on. Vehicles, pedestrians and shoppers at the fish market all scrambling for space, it resembled a second *Paul's Lot*. Back into normal clothes, the wig and print dress in my bag, I pushed my way to the bay for leeward vans. I was just in time to see *Valentine* pull in from a fresh run.

I watched the passengers climb out, and the grinning multi-coloured conductor collecting the fares. An overgrown boy in his mid-twenties, did he truly believe his job was the height of glamour? A passenger bumped into me, and for a while I lost the redhead. When I found him again, he was holding two bottles of Guinness reverently like an altar boy with two burning candles.

Being a good conductor, he knew his rank and place. So he served the driver before taking a sip of his drink. No problem, I said to myself, a cold beer on a boiling day, I was fine with that. What made me reach for my notebook was the quart bottle of *Sunset* rum that flashed on the dashboard. I could only shake my head as Leroy poured a measure into his Guinness, put the bottle to his head, and gulped hard and long.

A visit to the Baptiste shop was supposed to be next. Waiting patiently in the queue, I would get a glimpse of Barbara, and, if I was lucky, a few words. But when I checked my watch it was well after two. She would have to wait for another day, the rest of the afternoon belonged to me.

During our courting days, me and Joel used to visit Fort Charlotte. He would look out at the Bequia Channel and stare without blinking at the green-blue sea. What was he seeing that was invisible to me? Think back three hundred years, he would say, taking my hand and squeezing it tenderly. Imagine a ship capsizing in the channel somewhere about 1700, and the slaves swimming to Bequia.

It wasn't easy for me, I wouldn't lie. But bit by bit, after visiting Owia, Chateaubelair, Greiggs, Lacroix, Grand Sable and Sandy Bay, I started to look at SVG with new eyes. I began to see more than a place to bathe and eat and cook and drink. More than a country to sing and wind bad at carnival, parading your jewels, and stating your right to 'free up' once a year.

On each journey now I try to picture the women and men who once trod that very road. Ten years before, a hundred, twice that. Whenever my body feels restless, irritable, I would drive to Fort Charlotte and take myself back centuries. That Wednesday afternoon, I passed an hour there gazing at the tranquil waters, and came away feeling calm and refreshed.

On the way down from the Fort, my mind told me to wait till dark and pay the Veritys a visit. Not big and bold, but in a black outfit to blend with the night. I phoned Joel and explained my plan. He wanted to come with me, but he was in Fancy, a long drive away. I could handle things, I reminded him. He was disappointed, I could tell. But he knew I would look after myself for him.

The Verity family lived in Layou, high on a hill above the bay. Prime spot, way out of the Providence league. Leroy came home after seven. Bdm, Bdm, Bdm, that blasted music again, he was ten times worse than our neighbour. Couldn't he switch it off for a minute? I crept up to the side of the house in the darkness and sat there, breathing shallow, my ears cocked. A moaning noise came to me, a low argument, grunting, shouting. Then BBBBmmm!!! indoors, rattling the windows.

I squatted there all uncomfortable listening for what seemed like days. At last the front door opened. A smell of cologne hit me as Leroy climbed into *Valentine*. The engine kicked, and soon the van was tearing up the road.

I scrambled into the Toyota to follow. But there was no need to get close, the booming was like a magnet, it would drag me to his destination.

Leroy pulled up at a house in Camden Park. Small place,

nothing too grand. I saw him push open the door and stroll right in like the king in the arena. I sat in the car watching and straining my ears to listen. The crickets didn't help. Add in the mad fowls that couldn't tell dusk from dawn, and there was no chance of overhearing late-night chatter. Two hours later, when tiredness was really beginning to creep up on me, the music began to blast, *Valentine* was on the move once more.

Leroy didn't hurry now, I made it gone eleven when he got home. Layou was very quiet, and just as dark. A soft cry came to me in the darkness of the porch where I was stooping this time. Leroy shouting and Barbara crying, the pain and hurt in her voice were too much to bear. It was time to get home to my husband.

The next day it was back to Camden Park early, to check out the patient Leroy had paid an evening call. From the car I made out a yellow house. Two rooms, I guessed, with a small kitchen and a bathroom. I was thinking about asking a neighbour who lived there when a woman stepped out a side door.

The woman was wearing a purple top and tight white trousers that didn't reveal an inch of slack. She was cradling a basket of clothes. I watched her load the washing line with a child's vests and tiny trousers, five dresses, and two pairs of long black jeans. I waited till she was back inside, tiptoed to the house and rapped twice on the door.

Up close she looked young. If out of the teens, then not by much. A slender, pretty, young woman with the wide eyes you find in a girl before she turns into a woman proper. She had a strong, narrow face and straight, black, Indian hair. Under her white trousers she was wearing a red panty. Black under white is best, young lady, I had to stop myself saying, didn't your mother teach you anything?

'Yes?' Her voice was high-pitched, her face very annoyed.

'Mrs Cato?' I lobbed her the first name that came into my head.

She answered my question with a deep frown. 'No Mrs Cato living here.'

I pulled an A4 notebook from my bag and scrolled down imaginary names. 'You have a young daughter?'

The woman came back with, 'You from the Ministry of Health?'

'Yes,' I said, thankful for her help, 'we're checking on new mothers.'

She waved me in and pointed to a chair. 'Trust them to get the name wrong,' she scowled.

'Probably someone straight from training college,' I said. 'What name is it, then?'

'Ella.'

'Ella what?'

'Saunders.'

'Child's name?'

'Royella.'

'Surname?'

She didn't give it straight away, and when she did, she repeated, 'Saunders.'

I cast off the serious look and threw her my sweetest smile. 'I meant father's name. To make sure we get it right next time.'

Ella Saunders rubbed her chin with her right hand. 'I can't tell you that, Miss.'

I took her left hand in mine and stroked it gently. 'Just for our records.'

She spoke the name as though there was someone hiding in the bedroom who might overhear her. 'Leroy Verity.'

'How do you spell that?'

She took her time spelling the surname like a teacher guiding me through the alphabet. As I let go her hand to write,

I noticed a bruise near the elbow of her left arm, and a yellow scab. She caught me staring at it and turned her hand over quickly.

'How is Royella doing?' I asked. 'Creeping?'

'Walking,' Ella boasted. 'Two months now.'

'Eating well? Sleeping well?'

'Yes. The midwife signed me off.'

'Can I see her?'

The proud young mother nodded. She led me to the bedroom, small and roasting, even with the windows wide open. I saw the sleeping infant, beautiful, peaceful, her narrow naked back rising and falling with each breath.

'What about you Ella?' I asked when we were back in the hall. 'Everything fine with you?'

She took her time. 'Yes,' she answered, 'no worries.'

'*Healthy Mothers, Healthy Babies*,' I said in my most official voice, 'don't forget our slogan.'

But Ella Saunders was a woman now. She chirped her teeth.

'The midwife give me that speech already.'

I retaliated by pointing to the scab. 'That bruise, what happened?'

'The rain came off the sea just like that one afternoon, I rushed out to pick up the washing, and I fell down.'

I sighed out loud. 'The truth, Ella, or the Ministry will send out a nurse to check on you every day. They don't skylark when it comes to young mothers, you know.'

'I told you, I slipped.'

'Then how come the bruise was so deep?'

Tears began to form in her young eyes, and I couldn't help feeling sorry for her. She started to snivel.

'I was going to the shop three weeks ago to buy a soap, and someone attacked me.'

'Who?'

'I didn't see them.'

'Male or female?'

'Male.'

'How could you tell?'

'He was after my purse. Some of the bad boys in the area know Verity gives me real money, so he tried to rob me.'

'You reported the attack to the police?' I asked.

She shook her head.

'Verity said to leave it to him. He said he would find the culprit and deal with him.'

I got up to go. 'Look after yourself and Royella,' I said.

Over the next week I bounced between husband and wife. Barbara was back full time behind the counter, I bought health drinks for breakfast and lunch just to see her. When she served me, I grinned like a *Never-see-come-see* girl on her first visit to the capital. But the smile she could spare me always folded into a sad, haunted look. And the smile wasn't brighter when I watched her pick up her son from school. It was straight home for Mrs Verity, no time to discuss the rising price of fish with the other mothers.

But Leroy Verity was where my mind ended up when I switched from home life to the case. Van driver, big spender, music man, what kept him going?

He had stamina, no doubt about that. Late in night after night, I wondered how he managed to get up so early to begin his passenger run. Bursting with energy, admired by the other drivers, where was Barbara in his life? Was she happy at home while he worked, roamed and played?

My notes showed that he visited Ella Saunders at 2 p.m. on the Thursday two weeks into the case. Quick visit, to drop off a parcel. Work to home was his routine, and then a trip out later, to some bar with other drivers and conductors. But he stopped work at five on the Friday, paid the conductor his weekly wage, then drove to the Arnos Vale playing field.

A football squad was practising near the airport that evening, and making enough noise to drown out a small plane with their screaming. One of the female spectators should have joined the team. She was up and down the line bawling out instructions, all she needed was her football kit to score. As Leroy jogged from the pitch at the end of the session, she had a cold beer ready for his outstretched hand. Football coach or number one fan? When the players were in the showers, I spied her in the bar, so I went over.

The woman was in her mid-twenties, neat Caribbean-blend face, and short black hair combed out, not straightened: my kind of woman.

'Good team,' I said, sipping a fruit cocktail on expenses to her brandy.

She raised an eyebrow. 'You think so?'

Cricket was my sport, my knowledge of football was at the level below basic. But that didn't stop me when it came to my work.

'Good attacking play,' I replied. 'And solid defence.'

An open exercise book sat on her lap. I spotted a list of names, some with ticks, some with crosses.

'You're a team secretary as well?' she asked.

'Yes,' I answered, because I couldn't very well say no.

'Which team?'

I picked a name out of an imaginary hat. 'Richmond Rollers. Fancy a match sometime?'

She sipped her drink. 'I'll have to ask the boss.'

'Who's that?'

'Mr Verity.'

I straightened up. 'Leroy Verity?'

'Yes. It's his club. He buys the team kit, he stands the

match expenses out of his own pocket. You can't find a more generous man.'

'You know him well, then?'

'You can call it that.'

'So if I contact him for a fixture you think he might agree?'

The woman parked her glass on the counter and began to laugh. She squeezed her eyes shut, flung them open, and began to roar again. She laughed so hard and long I wondered whether I should quit as a PI and start touring the tourist hotels in the Grenadines as a comic.

'What's so funny?' I asked when the joke ran out of steam.

'Leroy is usually the one asking a woman for a fixture!' she answered.

'Has he asked you?'

She smiled, and I got the impression she would have been offended if he hadn't. 'Of course.'

'And?'

'I told him I would have to get permission from his wife.'

'What did he say to that?'

'He said he could fix things.'

'Meaning?'

'I don't know exactly. But they're splitting up or getting divorced: that's the talk among the players.'

I excused myself, said I was going to the bathroom, and crept out a side door.

The Baptiste family had a barbecue the following Saturday, and they invited me and Joel along. We were 'new suppliers' of arrowroot starch, and potential business partners. Tisha Jennings from Petit St Vincent, David Medica from New Grounds, and Norma Holder from Retreat, it was a pleasure to meet some of the people who kept the Baptistes in pole position with their mixtures.

You had to admire the passion of the growers. Each one

had a list of illnesses their blends could cure, some sensible, some you couldn't invent. Fruit drinks were the future, they had no doubt, sooner or later Caribbean people would come back to nature and 'discard the bottles and cans loaded with diabetes'. Their children ran about the yard tumbling, bouncing and screaming as we compared brews, can anything trump the laughter of happy children?

The house was a good size, and with a lawn to match. A square lawn like a boxing ring, I couldn't help thinking: Leroy at a table in one corner chomping and texting away, in the opposite corner, Mr Baptiste entertaining guests, but with his fighting gloves under the flannel he used to dry the back of his thick neck.

It was a good event, a hot day with a cooling breeze, and endless food and drink, as we say in SVG. At exactly one-thirty I saw Leroy take his son by the shoulder and run his fingers through his hair. Then he eased out of his chair and climbed into *Valentine*. No wave or nod to say he was off, I had my eyes on him, I didn't detect a sign.

Eli probably missed him, but no one else that I could see. You could feel the tension ease as *Valentine* boomed itself away. Barbara looked brighter now, not exactly smiley, but a happy host. I drifted over to where she was sitting having a rest and feeding her son.

'He's a handsome boy,' I said, taking the chair next to hers. 'What's his name?'

'Eli,' she said in her own time.

'How old is he?'

'Eight.'

Eli ran off to join the other children and, without him there, Barbara seemed a little lonely. I changed the subject.

'How did the business start?' I asked.

Barbara replied in the flat voice of a salesgirl in a Kingstown store I had no trouble recognising.

'My father came up with the idea. One Tuesday afternoon he ordered some health drinks for his training, the stuff in the shops was too sugary, so he decided to blend his own. Mom added hers, I did mine, by Sunday we had all the figures on paper to start the enterprise.'

'And it's just the three of you running it?'

'Yes. Me and mom in the shop, and dad up and down the mainland buying the ingredients, and across the Grenadines for the fruits we don't grow.'

'What about competitors?'

'None yet. But no doubt someone will jump onto our idea and grin in our face. That's what people do, isn't it?'

'And your strategies to fend them off? New brews? Marketing?'

'Sorry, I keep my files with the projections at home in the safe. Dad's idea: keep everything under lock and key.'

At last, an opportunity to visit the Veritys in daylight, instead of squatting and pressing my ears against a window.

'I'll drop by sometime next week,' I said. 'Barbados, Trinidad, Antigua and St Lucia, the overseas market must be crying out for your flavours.'

Barbara looked away, she seemed to find a boat out at sea more interesting than my suggestion. This was truly a woman with a lot on her mind.

'Probably Tuesday,' I added, because if I didn't fix a day, I was sure she would soon forget we ever met.

She didn't answer, she had shifted her gaze to the dust *Valentine* had stirred up. I left her and went to watch Joel sparring with her father.

I drove to Layou at five the following Tuesday. On the Monday I had double-checked with Barbara at the shop in town. Four o' clock, I promised, knowing full well I wasn't going to keep the appointment. For on Tuesdays Leroy usually shut down at six, I wanted to be there when he came home.

The house was beautifully furnished, Mrs Baptiste wasn't wrong. It was a good ten levels above the Providence home when it came to luxury and size. Barbara was dressed in a white blouse and loose faded jeans that hushed her Caribbean curves, she seemed happy to see me but a little nervous.

'Sorry Barbara,' I lied, 'my husband had the car.'

Her smile flashed then disappeared, but it was open, genuine. 'I understand, Mrs Providence,' she said. 'Not a problem.'

She pointed to the settee and took the armchair opposite. The rain and overnight thunder and lightning, the success of the barbecue, school and Community College, conversation flowed no problem. Barbara came across as a lovely woman, shy and sincere. But there was work to do. I was there to discuss pretend business, the sooner the better. So, placing my satchel on the floor beside me I said, 'Okay to get started?'

Barbara held up the palm of her left hand. 'Let me just check the dinner first. Verity should be on his way soon.'

She got up and went to the kitchen, and I watched her carefully, light steps, beautiful walk. A few minutes later she was back with two small bowls of steaming soup. She handed me one.

'Taste this for me,' she said, 'Verity doesn't like his food too peppery.'

I dipped the spoon, whistled away the steam, and sucked in the soup. Crayfish, a hint of garlic, flavour pepper, succulent eddoes, young green bananas, no doubt about the woman with the sweet hand.

'Your cooking is good,' I said. 'If I could make soup like this I would open a restaurant.'

I got my first lasting smile from Barbara. 'Thanks. It's good to be appreciated.'

She took her time eating, as good cooks do, searching for that extra ingredient for next time. As I waited for her to catch up I took in the pictures on the wall. Twelve, I counted, six of Eli, three of a super-cool Leroy dressed in his driving gear by the van, and three of Barbara, none recent.

'They're beautiful,' I said.

'Thanks.'

'Eli's tall, isn't he? How's he doing at school?'

'Pretty good. He likes English and Science, and he's quite a good runner.'

'Where is he?' I asked, knowing full well that I had asked his grandmother to keep him for the night.

'He's staying with my parents. My dad is teaching him to box.'

'Oh.'

'Do you have children, Mrs Providence?' Barbara asked.

Barbara's question caught me off guard: what she wanted to know, and the fact that she was asking at all. Mother Hendy was convinced I was 'holding back' something from Joel, whenever I was feeling low, I avoided her stall so I wouldn't have to explain that some women find it easier than others.

'Me and my husband are trying,' I found myself admitting to Barbara, and telling her about Mother Hendy.

'I understand,' she said with a sincerity that touched my heart. 'Keep trying, don't give up. Promise?'

Then, all of a sudden she began to cry. A gentle sniffle to begin with, but ending in a real bawl. I got up, took her hand and led her to the settee alongside me.

She cried, she trembled, she was like a child with a fever. I held her tight and told her she would be all right.

'Please forgive me Mrs Providence,' she begged when she was better, 'I'm weak, I shouldn't heap my burdens on a stranger.'

Six o'clock was approaching, I could see that she was getting panicky. Should I explain the true purpose of my visit, or wait till Leroy came home and hope that Lacy Luck had slipped in with him?

I took her hands, squeezed them gently, then told her, 'Barbara, I know about the problems you're having.'

She eased away her hands and looked at me.

'Do you?' She sounded sad, helpless, without a friend in the world.

'Yes. Your mother told me. She's really worried.'

She studied me for a while then said, 'Mother sent you here?'

'Yes.'

'Why?'

'I'm a private investigator, she hired me to help.'

'And my father?'

'She didn't want him to know: you can guess why.'

'*You* can't help me. No one can help me.'

'Why do you think that?'

'I've let things go too far, Mrs Providence. I should have walked out years ago, but I didn't. Where can I go now? Who would have me?'

When you take a battering round after round after round, I saw, man or woman, you can reduce yourself to the lowest negative.

'You're a good businesswoman,' I reminded her, 'you're clever, young, good-looking, the line of men queuing up to meet a woman with half your talents would stretch from here to the airport.'

She gave a half-smile, but even that didn't stay long. 'Those men will have to go through Verity first.'

'Every man is just a man, Barbara.'

I could hear now the fear in her voice. 'You don't know this one.'

'I used to be in the police force,' I tried to reassure her. 'We had to take on whatever or whoever came at us.'

A blast of music some moments later announced that Leroy had finished for the day. I took Barbara by the shoulders and squeezed her gently. 'Trust me,' I told her. 'But most of all, trust yourself.'

I had tried to keep the distance Sergeant Stoute drilled into us, but the moment Leroy stepped into the house, I could tell it was a battle I would lose. Every now and again me and Joel fell out, but he would never come in from work without greeting me. A grunt, perhaps, but a greeting all the same. What was I to make of a man who pushed open the door to his home, no word of greeting to the wife who had prepared his dinner, not even a nod to a woman who might be one of his wife's friends or a fellow businesswoman?

In less than a time Leroy had showered and changed into a white merino and blue shorts, and was sitting at the dining table like Daddy Bear. No music though, and I was thankful for this small mercy. I watched him pour a shot of rum into his bottle of Guinness, Little Tokyo all over again. Before he could empty the bottle, Barbara placed an enormous bowl of soup before him.

There was no 'Thank You', not even a glance up at his wife. Slurping the soup and texting with a vengeance was probably his way of showing his appreciation. Back in our seats I tried to keep Barbara's mind on the family business. All the while I kept an eye on Leroy, the man who was on my mind almost as much as my husband.

How long was he at the table, eight minutes, ten? I can't say exactly. When he had had enough he got up and disappeared into the bedroom, leaving bowl, spoon and bottle right where he had used them. A few moments later he came out, dressed in a red shirt and black jeans, and drowning in cologne. The round smooth face sprouted not a grain of hair, I could see why he was attractive to a certain type of girl.

Barbara gave me a pleading, desperate, look. Fear was in it, but hope too. I didn't answer the look. She had to make her own decisions.

'Verity,' she said to him, in a gentle voice.

Ignoring her, Leroy ran a comb through his hair and checked in at the closest mirror. I could see he liked what he saw.

'Verity, you went out last night, you can't leave me on my own again like this.'

The comb stopped in mid-brush. 'What?' Leroy bawled. 'What did you say?'

'We can't go on like this.'

Levi's eyes bulged. 'Since when you can tell me what I can and can't do, Barbara?' he howled.

'I know where you go at night, Verity, everybody knows.'

You could almost feel the heat from Leroy's nostrils.

'Barbara, you're lucky this person – whoever she is – is here, otherwise you would remember how to talk to me,' he bellowed.

'This person has a name, Mr Verity,' I said softly.

He wagged his right index finger at me and kept on wagging it. 'Name or no name, you keep out of our business, woman. I don't care who you are.'

'Cassie Providence,' I answered him gently but firmly. 'Remember it.'

Like a man who had better things to do than take women seriously, Leroy dismissed me with a chuckle and turned to his wife. 'I have business to fix, Barbara. When I come back I don't want to find this Providence woman here. Then you and me will have a *proper* conversation.'

He put the comb in his back pocket and made for the front door. Barbara got up from the settee and blocked him.

'Whaaaaat?' Leroy snorted. 'What the hell you think you doing, Barbara? You want trouble? Get the hell out of my way!'

Barbara didn't move. She had this hard, fierce look, no one was going to shift her. I went and stood on her right.

'Ha ahh ah!' Leroy brought up a huge laugh from the pit of his stomach. 'The two of you think you can match me?'

I didn't say anything, because I know that a laugh is never truly a laugh. Something is usually behind it. The instant you lower your guard your attacker spots a chance to pounce. I wasn't wrong. Another belly laugh, then Leroy suddenly hurled himself at us. A black and red blur, a huge trunk of flesh.

My police training came back to me, played at such a speed it was pure instinct. 'Get in to a hand-to-hand,' Sergeant Stoute would yell, 'get in close, you can't do damage from five feet away, but your attacker can.'

Getting in close cramps the attacker, his fists lose their power. So, as Leroy charged, swinging wild, I took a deep breath, pushed Barbara out of the way, and stepped in to meet him. Thump, phut, swush, my elbow took the blows, my forearm felt their sting too. But I bundled myself small, my eyes fixed on the target.

He had a good five inches over me. Long arms too, not to mention rage. I would have to make the first strike count, I realised, then follow up with a second blow. I might have to give a third, but I hoped it wouldn't come to that.

'You dirty, nasty tsincunk bitch!' Leroy snarled as his punches grazed my body, 'you think you bad?'

I ignored his Bajan, I soaked up the blows with my biceps. Now that I was in range, I opened the palm of my right palm and stiffened it. When I got a good view of Leroy, I struck him hard on the left side of his face with my palm.

I heard his teeth clatter. Even better, I saw his head tilt back from the blow. Now! Now! Deliver! I was aiming for his solar plexus when a wild punch struck me full on the lips, jamming them hard against my teeth.

It hurt. The punch set off a tingle, then my teeth, lips and mouth seemed to be on fire. I could taste warm blood, and feel a swelling that would take days to go down. Forget the blood, I told myself, ignore the tingling lips. Keep your eyes on Leroy, focus, wait. But now he was all over me, hurling blows at ten cents a dozen. I pulled myself in small again, took more hits on my back and my sides. Each hard knuckle hurt, my back was beginning to feel raw and hot. Shut down the pain, I reminded myself, stick to your plan! Trust Stoute!

The blows kept coming, each one loaded with an insult. But I waited. Waited, waited until Leroy's chin was exposed again. Yes! There! Right there! I flat-palmed him on the chin.

'Daahehehaaah!' he cried out, 'you stinking so-and-so!'

As his head jerked back, I got my palm ready again, like a *Goal Attack* about to shoot a netball. I went for the base of his nose this time and felt the satisfying flexing of gristle.

'You fushsckighnger!' Leroy grunted and snorted, he was mad. Better than that, he was off balance.

I reached up and grabbed his windpipe. He made a coughing, gurgling, choking sound. I tightened my grip. His hands reached for his neck to try to peel mine off him. This left him open, but before I could strike again, he drew back, and I felt a hard knee denting my stomach.

'Uughkgh.' The blow stunned me for a few seconds. It knocked out my breath and forced me to release my hold. 'Heuchugh.'

I coughed, bent over, and tried to soothe the pain in my stomach. I was vulnerable now, and Leroy could see it. He stopped swinging and made to dive at me.

'You know who you playing with?'

The kick was wearing off, my breath was slowly coming back. I saw the red and black blur about to charge me. Wait Cassie! Patience! Wait. The blow had knocked me back, so I had a few extra seconds to see Leroy clearly from where I was stooping. When he lunged now, I straightened up and stepped to the right. The woman he was aiming to grapple was now a ball of air. As his hands reached out for her, I delivered a karate chop to the back of his neck. And another. And a third to make sure.

I didn't need the last blow. Probably not the one before that either. For as the pain in my stomach was spreading, Barbara had grabbed a chair from the table and smashed it on Leroy's back. Once, twice, three times, I lost count at seven. Leroy tumbled like a new-born calf. Down he crashed, down, down, out. No more blows, no more swearing and cursing. Just a red and black heap on the floor.

Leroy flipped onto his back, as if his stomach wanted its share of blows too. I moved away, I was finished with him. For Barbara had taken my place, calm, hands by her side, as though she didn't know the word fear. Leroy looked up at her. Did he see her eyes? Did he understand what he was seeing?

Barbara placed her right foot on Leroy's chest. He seemed too stunned to move or say anything. Her face was a blank, the calmness in her was terrible to behold. She stayed like this for a minute, no words, just the glare, then she removed her foot. She walked away, leaving Leroy on his back. And there he stayed, like a man waiting for a magician to remove a spell.

Moments later, as he was getting to his feet, Barbara came back with the keys to his van.

'I hope the schoolgirl wants you, Leroy,' she said, flinging the keys at him, 'because I don't. Last night was the last night you slept in this house.'

Leroy picked up the keys from the floor and limped away.

Not long after, *Valentine* was eating up the road, no music, just the noise of the tyres stressing.

There wasn't much to explain to Mrs Baptiste when I went to see her on the Friday. Barbara had told her of the fight with Ella Saunders, the beatings from her husband, his refusal to have a second child with her. She was brighter now, Mrs Baptiste told me, little by little she was getting back to the Barbara of old. She thanked me, asked me to keep in touch, and handed me an envelope with a large bonus. She was happy the case was over, I was delirious that the swelling on my top lip was going down so I could kiss my husband properly.

Me and Joel were sitting taking in the sea breeze later that Friday evening when there was a soft rap at the door. Joel went to answer it, and came back with Barbara. She had a large flask of their latest drink, soursop, nutmeg and cinnamon. As we drank she kept staring at the two hammocks.

'Can I try one?' she eventually plucked up the courage to ask.

Joel nodded. 'Help yourself.'

She climbed into the smaller one – mine – and began to swing gently.

'This is real nice you now,' she said. 'Where did you buy it?'

'Buy?' Joel said with a frown. 'No way. Designed two, built two. And when I make a hammock, it's a proper hammock!'

'Can you build me one?'

'Let me get my tape measure to get your measurements,' he said, my husband, the champion hammock builder. 'Just tell me when.'

We had a few drinks, talked and laughed, and ate roast breadfruit and smoked herring. When we caught ourselves, the radio was announcing ten o'clock. Barbara excused herself. She was going to the bathroom before getting ready to go home, I assumed.

Five minutes later, when there was no sign of her, I went to check that she was all right. There was a tinkling noise in the kitchen, and I found her washing up glasses and dishes. I stood there watching her for a while then went back to Joel.

'What are you two doing Sunday?' she asked when she returned to us.

'Nothing,' I answered. 'Why?'

'I want to invite you to dinner. I was going to phone, but I prefer to do things in person.'

'We would love to.' Joel nudged me to remind me. 'But we're going up to the volcano – if the peak isn't too misty.'

'La Soufriere?' Barbara sounded excited rather than disappointed.

'Yes,' I said. 'But it depends on the weather in the morning.'

Her face was young again, bright, alive, excited. 'Can I come? Do you know, I've never been up to the crater!'

'It's an early start,' I explained, 'and you need the right clothes – and comfortable shoes.'

She felt the texture of her soft cotton blouse and looked down at her green maxi skirt. Her eyes lifted to me, and I could see her mind working.

'Me and you are about the same size Cassie,' she said. 'You must have something I could wear.'

I took her hand.

'Come. Let's go and see what we can dig up.'